GENERAL BESSERLEY'S
SECOND PUZZLE BOX

GENERAL BESSERLEY'S SECOND PUZZLE BOX

By

E. PHILLIPS OPPENHEIM

BOSTON

LITTLE, BROWN AND COMPANY

1940

CONTENTS

GENERAL BESSERLEY'S
SECOND PUZZLE BOX

I

THE DUCHESS GAVE A PARTY

GENERAL BESSERLEY sat before his writing-table, drawn close up to the wide-flung windows of his summer-house, his pen clasped in his idle fingers, his eyes wandering though a tangle of drooping roses and clematis beyond the gardens below to where a car was crawling up the mountain road. He leaned a little sideways and touched a bell. In a few moments a white-coated butler opened the door and approached the table.

"It is, I believe, *Madame la Vicomtesse* who arrives, Henri," his master announced. "Send word to Jean that the gates may be opened and let François know that there will probably be a guest for lunch."

"*Parfaitement, Monsieur.*"

The servant departed. General Besserley laid down his pen and stood in the entrance to his exquisitely planned summer retreat. He watched the car, now clearly visible, took note of the familiar uniform of the chauffeur, recognized the single slight figure of the woman seated in the corner of the limousine toying with her sunshade. It was a morning of early springtime, before the sweetness had been drawn from the flowers or the colour from the herbage. Even though this was France, there were birds singing. The blue expanse of the distant Mediterranean glittered in the sunshine, but Besserley, so responsive as a rule to all the beautiful sights and sounds and perfumes by which he was surrounded, looked only at the woman. The car swept through the open gates and came suddenly to a standstill. The Vicomtesse de Bressac, once known as Lady Grace Massingham, the most popular woman in Monte Carlo, descended with the air of one in familiar surroundings and climbed the little footpath towards the Chalet. Besserley stepped forward to meet her.

"Once more, my dear Grace!" he exclaimed, as he bent over her fingers. "I am so happy to see you."

She smiled and the natural gaiety of a girl was there still in her expression of obvious delight.

"They told me in Paris that you were here," she said. "Victor said you were on no account to be disturbed — that you had really begun your Reminiscences."

"The writing of those Memoirs is only my excuse to gain a little solitude," he told her. "Solitude, as you know very well, means only a refuge from boring people. You will lunch, of course?"

"May I?" she asked.

He waved the car on to the Château which loomed in the background and led his visitor into the Chalet. Here he established her in his favourite easy chair and hurried Henri away with his special orders.

"You flatter me, Grace, you know, by this prompt visit," he said.

"My dear man," she replied, "I am like everyone else. I do the thing I like best in life. As it hap-

4

pens, though, I come also upon a serious errand."

He shook his head at her.

"Nothing in this world could bring me to a gala dinner."

"You are ungallant!" she exclaimed. "I have only one reply — nothing in the world would induce me to invite you to one."

"We all have our weaknesses," he excused himself. "My work —— "

She interrupted him with a laugh.

"The only time I have seriously doubted the genuineness of your sense of humour," she said, "is when you show your aversion so pointedly to those harmless and pleasant little functions. Never mind, I came to see you upon something that really matters. I must have your advice, and at once. I may even have to ask you to fight a duel for me."

"You know how I hate bloodshed," he sighed, "but it shall be done."

Henri appeared with a tray. She accepted her cocktail with a little gesture of delight.

"Now," she declared, "I shall feel fortified, because really, Sam, I am in trouble and I need your help."

"Come out into the garden for a few moments," he proposed, "whilst they lay the table here."

He led her to a seat in a retired spot. She certainly showed then that she could be a woman of plain speech.

"Sam," she confided, "that Dragounil woman has given up her establishment in Paris, she is opening up her villa here and commencing operations next month.

Nothing will keep Maurice away from the villa, the stories of his losses will get into the Press, his grandfather will keep his word. He will be ruined — incidentally, so shall I."

"Very concisely put," Besserley acknowledged with a sympathetic smile. "It follows without saying that the wicked Duchess must not open that villa."

"She owns it, you know," Grace reminded her companion. "How is one to stop her?"

"Problems in my young life," he replied, "I have solved by the dozen but never yet have I been able to solve them on an empty stomach. You see the mystic signs behind? Our omelette is being served. Put this little matter out of your mind for an hour, Grace. Afterwards we will see what can be done."

"Almost you inspire me to hope," she murmured as she passed her hand through his arm.

They lunched before the open window, to the music of a few isolated feathered songsters and the faint sighing of the west wind in the pine trees. François, the chef, presented himself for a moment to pay his respects to his master's honoured guest. He doffed his tall white headgear and bowed low.

"*Madame la Vicomtesse est servie avec une omelette fines herbes*," he announced. "*Après cela la truite de rivière de ce matin et puis les petites côtelettes d'agneau, très très petites, avec les petits pois et pommes de terre sautés. Pour finir vous avez un soufflé et comme vin le Montrachet 'vingt-et-un et le Château Mouton Rothschild 'seize.*"

"*C'est parfait*, François," the Vicomtesse acknowledged, smiling.

François bowed low; he bowed also to his master, who nodded his commendations, and took his leave.

"It is an old custom of François'," Besserley apologized. "He hates the menu. He likes to announce his performances."

"Already I forget my troubles," Grace declared as she took her place.

Luncheon amply fulfilled its promise. With the coffee, cigarettes and a not too heavy Armagnac were served. Then Besserley opened his desk, ran through some papers and drew out a gilt-edged glossy card.

"The Duchess opens her villa, I see, on the twentieth of next month," he remarked.

"You, too, are marked down for a victim! You are going?"

"I had no idea of accepting," he replied. "I don't approve of heavy gambling in private houses. What you are telling me, though, may make a difference."

"Give me some advice," she begged earnestly. "Tell me what to do. You know the story of Maurice's life up to now. He has lost twenty-five millions and both his châteaux — gambling. His grandfather allows him now a quite adequate income upon one sole condition — that he never enters a casino or indulges in heavy gambling anywhere. He will go to this woman's villa and he will lose as he always loses. She has had some of his millions already. His grandfather will hear

7

about it and it will be the end. It will be the end of a great family, Sam. Even though our marriage has been rather a pitiful affair, I do feel my responsibilities."

Besserley was silent for several moments. He rose to his feet and moved to the threshold of the Chalet, looking down at the smiling valley below. His heart was full of sympathy for the woman who had broken through her proud silence to make this appeal, but the pain he felt was not for her alone.

"I can give you no advice, Grace, for the moment," he said, turning towards her. "Don't communicate with his grandfather, whatever you do. I will make some enquiries. We shall meet again often, I hope, before the villa opens. I may have to go to Paris. If I do, I shall see Maurice. I will do all that I possibly can to help you."

Her eyes were a little sad, even though she knew so well the reason for his constraint.

"You will find him entirely and absolutely hopeless," she declared. "He will not call playing at the villa gambling at all. Such rubbish!"

"I shall not argue with him," he told her. "I know myself how obstinate a family the De Bressacs are. Something else may occur to me."

They loitered over their coffee, they walked for a while in the flower gardens and back through the pine grove. It was late in the afternoon before Besserley handed his guest into her car.

"A memorable afternoon, dear Grace," he said. "If

8

I see any hope — and I shall see hope — I will let you know. You must trust me."

"You are a marvellous man. You seem to help everyone who is in trouble," she sighed, as he raised her fingers to his lips. "I hate tearing myself away."

"And I shall loathe going back to my Memoirs," he assured her.

The car rolled away and Besserley climbed the rock-hewn steps and found his way back to his Chalet. The name of Besserley appeared in no telephone directory, but with a key which hung from a chain in his pocket he unlocked the door of a mahogany cabinet where an instrument was disclosed, asked the exchange for a number in Paris and walked backwards and forwards in the quickly passing twilight until he was called. He spoke for some time in English. Then he asked for another number and entered upon a very guarded conversation in French. He wound up having arranged a rendezvous, rang off and moved back to his task. He read over the last sentence he had written of his manuscript and sighed as he enclosed the sheet in a leather folder and packed it away. The world was destined to wait a little longer for those much discussed Memoirs.

For several weeks the distinguished figure of General Besserley was seen in strange parts of Paris. He was a frequent visitor at a little Bureau of Information situated in the Boulevard Haussmann, a bureau which had an anomalous existence and was supposed to be the possession and hobby of a well-known foreigner. He frequented even stranger places. He visited a famous sporting club where there was a good deal of gambling behind closed doors, and he even crossed the river and travelled down to one or two of the factories engaged in the manufacture of billiard-tables, factories which supplied casinos all over the world with the impedimenta of their trade. He made a few strange acquaintances and gained a vast amount of miscellaneous but thoroughly useful knowledge concerning the day-by-day life of croupiers, professional gamblers and their kind. He met Maurice de Bressac, Grace's husband, one day at the Armenonville before the racing and they lunched together.

"I saw your wife only a fortnight ago," Besserley told his companion. "She looked just as charming as ever — a little worried about you, as usual."

The young man's attractive but boyish face clouded over.

"I do wish she would let me run my own affairs," he said peevishly. "If I choose to drop a little money gambling she worries about it as though we had not a *sou* left in the world."

"Steady, now," Besserley remonstrated kindly. "It is not a little you lose, remember. It is a great deal, even when you have a millionaire grandfather behind you. She is a sensible woman and she would much rather see you settle down. Gambling's a mug's game, after all, you know."

"That depends entirely upon whether you have any

10

luck or not," the young man declared cheerfully. "You gamble yourself, sometimes, do you not?"

"Occasionally," Besserley replied. "I do it just as I should pay a subscription to a very expensive club. One meets at the casinos all one's friends, there are to be found there the best restaurants, the best dancing and a certain amount of excitement for one's money. All the same, gambling for large sums is stupid. You must lose in the long run."

"That is an old woman's wail," he laughed. "Take the simplest game — roulette. Thirty-six numbers and zero, and they give you thirty-five to one against any number you like. If you have a little luck you must win sometimes. If you have a lot of luck you might win some weeks or some months practically the whole of the time. The odds in all these games of chance are not much more against you. You have a fair run for your money and if you have the instinct for it, gambling is the greatest amusement in the world. Racing does not amuse me. I know very little about horses and I can never reckon up what the odds are against me. Gambling on the tables I can figure out exactly."

"Oh, I suppose, if you want to throw your money away," Besserley conceded, "and if you are sure that you are getting a fair run for it, the tables are the best."

"I wish someone would make Grace see that. She and my grandfather between them make me perfectly sick sometimes. I admit I have lost a few million francs, but why should they try to stop the only thing that really amuses me in life? My grandfather can afford it well enough. He has had to pay my debts once or twice, of course, but that is because he does not make me a sufficient allowance."

"I don't think you would find any trouble about the allowance if you were to settle down and chuck the casinos of your own will, for good," Besserley assured him.

"Why should I? Gambling is the only thing, as I said before, that amuses me. I shall put fifty *mille* on a horse this afternoon, and I shall not understand why I win or why I lose, and except for the money, it will not give me any particular pleasure. If I take fifty *mille* into a casino, I know exactly where I am the whole of the time. Let us stop talking about it, Besserley. Do not forget you are coming up to shoot with us next season. The old man is all the time talking about the way you picked off those tall pheasants at Rambouillet."

"Very nice of him," Besserley acknowledged smiling. "When are you coming south?"

"Well, you have asked me and I will tell you," the young man replied a little stubbornly. "I am going down for the opening of the Dragounil villa next week. I shall not stay with Grace because I know she will try to persuade me that gambling in a private house on a big scale is the same as a casino."

"You will have your own way, I suppose," Besserley remarked. "As you say, as long as you get a fair run for your money you may get your losses back in time. All the same, if you will take a word of advice from an older man, you will keep your losses out of the paper. You would feel foolish, wouldn't you, if anything were to happen to the old man and you found yourself a Marquis of France instead of just a humble Vicomte and about fifty thousand francs a year to keep the estates up on? Those elderly gentlemen are peculiar, you know."

The young man laughed.

"I am not afraid," he declared stubbornly.

"I will leave you to it, then," Besserley said, "unless you are ready. The first race is at two-thirty, and I have a *mille* on an American-bred horse."

"I will come with you."

"Toss you for the bill?"

"Good."

Besserley tossed and lost.

"Glad you can win sometimes, young fellow," he said as they strolled off.

Besserley travelled down to the Riviera a few days later in a somewhat depressed frame of mind. His work in Paris had produced results of a sort, but it was a malodorous business and even now there was no certainty about it. He slept the night in the train, and a bath as soon as he reached the Château and a change into light flannel clothes made a new man of him. He strolled down the terraces to his Chalet, unlocked the telephone cabinet and rang up Grace. She gave a little cry of pleasure as she recognized his voice.

"My dear man," she exclaimed, "where have you been?"

"Paris," he answered, "and not very happy about it. I am back now, though. The gardens are more beautiful than ever."

"And the Memoirs?"

"I need inspiration. If you tell me that you are lunching out, I shall be in despair."

"I was, but I am not. I am coming to you. I will be there at half past twelve. Fortunately, I was lunching at the Country Club after golf and I can easily arrange that."

"One anxiety removed," Besserley replied with a sigh of relief.

"Can we have luncheon not later than one, please?" she begged. "I am going over to play backgammon with Miss Talbot early this afternoon. She is such a dear and a confirmed invalid now."

"Luncheon shall be ready on the tick," he promised.

He rang for his secretary and went lazily through his letters seated outside in a low chair, a happy man again in the country and surroundings he loved. Soon it was all over. His work was concluded by signing a few cheques, notes of regretful excuse to a score of invitations and acceptances to about half a dozen. The secretary returned to the Château with his portfolio under his arm. Besserley relaxed and listened to

14

the bees, watched the butterflies and the fluttering petals falling from the fruit trees in the orchard. There were cows there moving lazily about and the pleasant rhythm of a reaping machine was in his ears. He sat up at last with a little start.

"At heart I believe I am a hedonist," he acknowledged to himself. "I ought to be thinking about Thursday night and I can't . . ."

He strolled down to the gate as soon as the car appeared. Grace sprang out and hurried up the slope towards him.

"Oh, my dear, what a time you have been away!" she exclaimed.

"And what happiness to be back!" he replied.

She told him the local news and of the parties during his absence. They compared notes about their gardens and disputed mildly on the subject of herbaceous borders. It was not until the cocktails arrived that he even referred to Paris.

"I saw your husband at the Armenonville," he told her. "We lost a little money together at Longchamps. No, I'm wrong, I think he won."

"Well?" she asked expectantly.

"Oh, I didn't do much in the way of a frontal attack," he confided. "We both talked the usual platitudes and agreed to differ."

"Is he coming down?"

"Yes."

"I haven't heard."

"He is going to the Carlton."

She sighed.

"That's bad news," she said.

He peered into the shaker and divided the remainder of its contents.

"You must know, Grace," he told her, "that I didn't go to Paris with the idea of coming the elderly gentleman over Maurice and stuffing him full of good advice."

"You are not elderly," she declared indignantly.

"Getting that way or the almanack lies," he replied smiling. "I shall have to ask you to be lenient with me, dear, because the situation is very difficult, a little precarious, and I dare say I have made a darned idiot of myself. Still, I have some influence in various directions, and I tried to make use of it. I cannot even prophesy the result but I have done what I can. You will believe that, won't you?"

"My dear, I think it is wonderful," she confessed, taking his hand. "I won't ask you a single question. I always remember what you said when I asked you once to do something for me when you had an official post in Paris. 'If it is possible, it shall be done. If it is impossible, it still shall be done.' Now, I don't think it is possible for you to stop Maurice going to the Duchess' or to stop him from losing money when he gets there, but if there is any way, I know that you will have thought of it."

"And so to lunch," he concluded.

He spoke no more of the matter until he handed her

16

into her car. Then he asked her a rather abrupt question.

"Are you going to the villa Thursday night?"

"Just as you advise," she replied. "Everyone whom we know on the Riviera is going and I dare say a great many others. I gain nothing by staying away, and it is just possible if I am there that it may have some slight effect upon Maurice."

"Then come," he said.

The memory of the opening of the Villa Dragounil and the great party given by the Duchess to commemorate the occasion was probably the most amazing episode that the Riviera had ever known. At nine o'clock, dinner was served to a hundred guests in the large dining-room. The ante-room adjoining it had also been furnished with small tables at which about sixty were seated in parties of four. Between the reception-room and the dining-room was the salon which was to be devoted to play. The cars outside reached the whole of the way in one direction to Cannes and in the other to Golfe Juan, and a force of forty gendarmes was necessary to keep any sort of order. The minor arrangements had all been made by the Duchess and her secretaries with her usual skill. It was insisted upon that everyone should bring their invitation cards — the black ones alone were for dinner, and until the guests holding these had arrived and taken their places, the cars with the rest of the world invited only to the reception and subsequent gambling were not allowed to deposit their passengers. At a quarter past nine, dinner was being served to one hundred and sixty people. Soon after ten, a further stream of cars began to arrive with guests who were shown into the reception-room on the other side. The gambling room was locked from the dining-room end, also by the door leading into the lounge, and occupied at first only by the croupiers and a couple of professional money-changers. The scene was rightly described as a brilliant one, for the tall windows of the room designed for the gambling were thrown open, and these led on to the terrace with the swimming-pool below and the sea. The guests who came only to the reception were received by a relation of the house and served with such refreshments as they desired from a huge bar in a small room opening out from the apartment. At eleven o'clock it had been announced that a gong would be struck and the doors leading into the salon set aside for gambling would be opened simultaneously from the lounge and the dining-room. Everyone was on tiptoe with expectation as the time drew near. Maurice de Bressac, who was with his wife in the lounge, could scarcely conceal his excitement.

"I wonder where old Besserley is," he asked her once. "I thought he was coming."

"He was invited to the dinner," Grace told him.

"He would not go," Maurice declared. "He is a broadminded sort of chap in his way, but he does not like the Duchess. Never said a word to me about her,

18

but I know it. What a party to give — this. Only two
baccarat-tables," he groaned, "and no chance of re-
serving seats here. . . ."

It was still half an hour before the time fixed for the
sounding of the gong when the Duchess' steward of
the household, an elderly man who had in his younger
life served no one but royalty, entered the dining-room
as pale as a ghost and approached his mistress. He
leaned over and whispered in her ear. The Duchess
frowned.

"But how can I hear what you say, Paul?" she
remonstrated. "What is the matter with you? Are
you ill?"

"Your Grace —— " he faltered.

He would have fallen down at that moment but the
man who was seated on the Duchess' right hand caught
his arm and held him up. He collected himself with
an effort.

"Your Grace," he faltered, "the *Commissaire* of
Police and a company of gendarmes are in the *Salle
des Jeux*."

The Duchess, too, changed colour, though she was
anything but pale. With a stare of blank bewilder-
ment she rose to her feet in a fury.

"How dare they intrude here?" she exclaimed.
"Prince, I must ask you to excuse me for a moment.
Something inexplicable has happened. Monsieur de
Fougranes," she went on, addressing the man on her
left, "be so good as to take my place. The gong will
be sounding directly for you to come into the *Salle*

des Jeux. I am wanted for a moment and I must leave you."

Her distinguished guest bowed and took the Duchess' place. She herself was, with a graceful gesture, to have unlocked the door leading into the *Salle des Jeux*, and the key was in her bag. She opened the door and passed in — the steward behind her. She was accosted almost at once by the Chief *Commissaire* of Police of the district. She looked around her in amazement. The room seemed full of gendarmes.

"What is the meaning of this?" she demanded furiously.

"Your Grace," the *Commissaire* replied, "I am not myself wholly informed, but this I do know. We have instructions from Paris to examine the gaming-tables at which you propose to entertain your guests and to search and cross-question the croupiers whom you have engaged. We must proceed with our task."

The Duchess, a tall, handsome woman, preserved her composure.

"This," she pronounced, "is the most idiotic outrage I have ever heard of. Paul," she added to the steward, "have the gong sounded. Let my guests come and see what this pantomime means."

The steward bowed and took his leave. Almost immediately the great gong hung up outside was beaten, the door of the lounge was opened and a stream of people flowed in from either side. At the sight of the gendarmes there were screams, cries of amazement, a babel of voices of all sorts. Everyone demanded an explanation. The Duchess, quite cool, stood in the middle of the room.

"I have no idea what this means," she confessed. "*Monsieur le Prince*," she went on, turning to the man who had been seated on her right, "perhaps the *Commissaire* can explain to you. He speaks about having authority to examine these tables."

The *Commissaire* looked round. The situation was becoming incredible. Suddenly, Besserley, who had slipped out of the crowd, touched him on the shoulder and whispered in his ear. The *Commissaire* nodded and held up both his hands. By degrees the clamour of voices ceased. The *Commissaire* had a mighty voice, and he used it to good effect.

"*Messieurs et Mesdames*," he announced, "an order has come to the Chief of Police here to inspect the gaming-tables placed in this apartment. I am here to carry out the orders for my superiors. I beg that you will accept the explanation which I give you of our presence here. You are free to come and go as you will, provided you do not obstruct my men in their duty. Make a circle around the two baccarat-tables," he ordered the sergeant of gendarmes. "Keep the people away from the tables. Inspector, bring that croupier to me."

There was silence now — a great breathlessness seemed to become almost an audible sensation. People found their way into the room by other means. It was soon crowded. The inspector passed his hand over the croupier, a small man who struggled and fought

21

at first but submitted afterwards in a sort of coma. From an inner pocket the inspector produced two half packs of cards. One was wholly composed of eights and one of nines. He turned to the Duchess.

"Your Grace," he said, "I ask you to observe these cards which I have taken from the pocket of your *chef de baccarat*. Here," he went on, stooping down to the floor by his side, "is the 'shoe' presumably to be used to-night. It has, as you will observe, a false bottom connected with the handle by a spring."

The Duchess was pale now but the look of horror on her face was unmistakable.

"You do not connect me with this horrible affair?" she asked. "You are not suggesting that I engaged a croupier and gave my sanction for the use of his cheating appliances?"

The inspector made no reply. He put the cards in his pocket and the "shoe" he handed to a gendarme.

"Remove that croupier," he ordered. "Take him to the station."

The man was marched out of the room. The croupier at the other baccarat-table was dragged up. He, too, had cards in his pocket. His "shoe," too, had the same device. He followed his companion in misfortune without saying a word. Two or three of the gendarmes who had been under the roulette-table were called by the *Commissaire*.

"Any report?" the latter asked.

"The roulette-table," the inspector explained, "is

fitted with the same device as the one found and broken up years ago in Marseilles. The device is apparently not completed but it only needs a little more fixing."

The *Commissaire* repeated the inspector's words. The latter continued.

"The device has been described in several magazines. The croupier can influence the falling of the ball into one particular quarter of the board. That is all the control he has over it but it is sufficient to ensure winning or losing."

The *Commissaire* repeated the report.

"I may say," he went on, "that the man who has examined the roulette-board is an expert sent down from Paris and not one of my staff. Your Grace —— "

He was unable to continue his sentence. The Duchess had fainted. Two or three of the men led her from the room. Besserley touched the *Commissaire* again on the shoulder.

"What are your further instructions, *Monsieur le Commissaire?*" he asked.

"We are to make no arrests, *Monsieur le Général,*" was the reply. "We are to lock up the room in which these tables are and leave them for the inspection of an emissary from headquarters who is flying down in the morning. I shall remove my men now, *Monsieur le Général.* I am very sorry to have been the unhappy means of spoiling everyone's enjoyment, but our information doubtless saved them a great deal of money."

It seemed as though there was going to be a very

tame and strange ending to what was without doubt the most flamboyant tragedy the gambling world had ever known. Everyone was talking in excited whispers, into which, little by little, crept a note of indignation. The *Commissaire* whispered to the inspector and saluted the company.

"If everyone will kindly leave this room," he said, "we propose to lock it up."

The excited guests were pushed back into the dining-room and into the lounge. The four doors were locked. There was a riot of voices, then suddenly a shout. Maurice de Bressac was the ringleader. In five minutes the door leading into the lounge was broken through. The crowd who had been in the dining-room came streaming in from the gardens.

"Keep the women away!" Maurice de Bressac called out. "We are going to get something out of the evening, anyway."

Then for a time pandemonium reigned.

"Into the swimming-pool!" Maurice cried. "Down the chute here. Smash 'em up! Smash every bit. Tear off the cloth."

With every sort of imaginable weapon which the men could find, dragged from all over the house, they set upon those tables. The first baccarat-table went slithering down into the pool a complete wreck, with the green baize cloth hanging around it and two legs missing. Then, as weapons became more plentiful, destruction was quicker. The roulette-table took forty men to move, but it went at last with the others toppling down with a mighty splash into the pool. Besserley found Grace and took her by the arm.

"I can find my car," he said. "No good talking to Maurice now. I'll take you home."

She clung to him as they fought their way through the crowd. Even before they reached the road, Besserley's chauffeur accosted them. The car was there waiting. Grace stepped into it and sank back amongst the cushions. Perhaps, of all the reactions of that strange night of mingled passions and volcanic disturbances, her reaction was the strangest. She covered her face with her hands and sobbed violently. Her hand felt for Besserley's and gripped it. So they drove off, metre by metre, until at last they reached the open route. The car swung almost at right angles and commenced to climb the mountain road.

"Where are we going?" she asked suddenly.

"You are coming home with me," he replied, "for a time, at any rate. I am not sending you back alone to that great empty house of yours."

She stole a glance at him. His face was set and rigid and he was watching the road.

"To-night was your doing?" she asked.

"Partly," he acknowledged. "The Dragounil woman has had those rascally croupiers and the doctored table for five years. The police refused to believe it or to act, but I had influence and I forced the matter through. You came to me in despair, you asked me to help you and this was the only way."

She looked away and he knew she was crying softly.

Her fingers, however, tightened upon his. They drove up to the Chalet, which was brightly illuminated. Henri hurried down.

"You planned this?" she whispered.

"I thought we had better have a shelter," he replied.

She took his arm and mounted the steps. At the top, a little table had been placed outside. There was wine and food prepared, caviare in a silver tub, a gold-foiled bottle, even cocktails. Slowly rising below them was a deep orange-coloured moon. All between them and the sea was like a scene out of fairyland.

"Well, here we are," he said in a suddenly matter-of-fact tone. "Shall we have supper served at once?"

"A few minutes," she begged. "Tell him to take them inside," she went on, pointing to the cocktails. "I — I am out of breath. It is the climb and all this excitement."

She held his hands and her fingers were icy cold. She led him up into the room.

"Dear," she whispered, "before anything else happens — before we sit down, I am going to thank you. What you have done is wonderful. And think of the joy I am feeling. You did it for me. Stoop down, please."

She drew his face to hers and kissed him tenderly, a woman's full-meaning, glorious embrace. It seemed to her that she had been saving that kiss all her life. It seemed to him that he had been waiting for it.

"That is because I love you and I thank you," she said, drawing away at last breathless. "There."

26

. . . Henri served them with a wonderful supper. Before it was half-way through they saw brilliant lights flashing up the road and across the country already bathed in moonlight. They watched them.

"It is Maurice," she said, and her voice was cold and far off.

He sprang from the car when he saw them in the avenue and came up the steps at a young man's flying pace. He went straight to Grace and took her hands in his.

"I followed you, dear," he said. "I had to. Besserley, was this your doing?"

"Partly," Besserley admitted.

Maurice held out his hand.

"I cannot tell you how grateful I am," he said. "Listen to me, please. Here is my pledge. I give you, my wife, my word as a De Bressac upon my honour that I will never gamble again except you are by my side, and I will never gamble for one franc more than you permit. You see, I am going to make my oath an oath that can be kept. Besserley, I make you the same promise."

"Another place, Henri," Besserley ordered, accepting the young man's hand. "Come and join us, Maurice," he invited.

II

THE GREAT Domiloff himself, the dictator of all Monte Carlo, touched Besserley on the arm as he was watching a crowded roulette-table in the Sporting Club. Besserley strolled away with him.

"I would not have disturbed you, General, if you had been playing seriously," he said, "but there is a fellow in the bar who wants to meet you particularly, and I think he might interest you. He has one of the quaintest notions I ever heard of — wants to open a bureau here in the Principality to sell stocks and shares."

"Doesn't sound good," Besserley remarked.

"Well, I like to be civil to everyone to start with," Domiloff went on, "and he certainly has nice manners. He has a daughter with him — a quiet little thing, but plays excellent tennis."

"Unusual appendage for a sharepusher," Besserley, who was not in the best of tempers, observed.

"I do not know that he is that," his companion reflected doubtfully. "He looks more like a clergyman on holiday than anything."

Besserley was himself somewhat impressed by the agreeable and well-dressed stranger who was presently introduced to him as Mr. Homfret. He was a middle-aged man of pleasant and cultivated speech. His hair was beginning to turn grey, but he carried himself

28

well and had rather the air of one who had lived an out-of-door life. His features were certainly good and there was nothing in the least sinister in his expression. The three men talked for a few minutes on indifferent subjects, then Domiloff was called away and Homfret, with some slight show of nervousness, drew his chair a little nearer to his companion's.

"I have only been here a few days, General," he said, "but everyone has told me that if one wants to know anything about Monte Carlo or the Riviera generally, you are the man to go to. I have an idea at which Baron Domiloff laughs, but I still believe in it."

"Let's hear it," Besserley suggested.

"Well, I don't claim to be a philanthropist," Homfret began, "but the idea did come to me first thinking about others. You know, you see so many of these young fellows coming down here, and old ones, too, for that matter, and they win heavily and then go away beggars, their holiday spoilt and hating the place. You know why, I suppose?"

"They go on playing," Besserley ventured.

"You've got it first time," his companion assented with a pleased smile. "That's just it, General. If people had the sense to leave off when they have made a good win and get away with it, they would have a chance of keeping their money and being the better for it. Now, I was in the bank here when I first came down and they have a room there which is connected up with London and New York, and a dozen clients sitting around just like an ordinary American bucket shop. Well, that showed me that there were plenty of people here who think of making money apart from the gambling side of it. I have a little capital and it occurred to me it would be quite a scheme to open a small business as a dealer in bonds and watch here for these fellows who have had a pretty good win, go to them and persuade them, on the spot, to invest their money."

Besserley smiled.

"You would find it a little difficult, I think," he remarked.

"I'm not so sure," was the eager reply. "That feeling of wanting to go on playing is not so strong when you have first touched money and made a win. My idea is that a good many people would be very glad to put their money somewhere where they couldn't get at it for a time and by degrees the desire to play again would wear off."

"It is not such a bad scheme," Besserley, whose temper was a little improved by a whisky and soda, admitted. "I can imagine people of sound common sense like you or myself being attracted by it. I don't know about these youngsters, though. By the by, is the young lady looking for you?"

"My daughter," Mr. Homfret said, rising to his feet and beckoning.

She came across to their table. She was still in tennis kit, a quiet but attractive-looking girl, with beautiful eyes and a slim, athletic figure. Besserley liked the humorous curve of her lips and her complete naturalness. She sat down between them and asked for a lemon squash, spoke for a few minutes of the tennis, then turned to Besserley with a smile. She was very much better looking when she smiled.

"Has Father been trying to sell you any bonds?" she asked.

"Not yet," Besserley replied. "Is he likely to?"

"I don't know how long you have known him. He has just taken up the idea that he would like to sell bonds or shares to people who have been winning at the tables, and whenever he has a new idea he can't as a rule keep away from it. Can you, Dad?"

"This is scarcely the place to discuss such a matter," her father admitted, "unless I had been introduced to General Besserley as a large winner. Then I think I should be acting the part of a philanthropist if I tried to persuade him to exchange his *mille* notes for gold bonds."

"I am not sure that you are likely to be very popular with the authorities here — Baron Domiloff, for instance," the girl observed. "From what I have seen of them I think they like to keep the money in the family."

"I think so, too," Besserley agreed. "I am rather surprised at Domiloff taking an interest in it, anyway."

"I don't think it will ever come to anything — like a good many of my father's ideas. He is always trying something new, you know, General Besserley. . . . Is that your Château that one can just catch a glimpse

31

of up in the mountains above the Gourdon Gorges?"

"That's where I live," he admitted.

"You are a long way away from all the life and excitement of this place," she remarked a little wistfully.

"Monte Carlo is very attractive," Besserley said, "but it is a good place to get away from sometimes. Besides, I do some work in my spare time."

"My daughter is quite an artist," Mr. Homfret confided. "She divides her time between tennis and sketching."

"Two very agreeable occupations. You are well-situated here for both: heaps of picturesque places to visit and the best tennis in the world."

"That's why I would rather like Dad to open up his old bond-shop," the girl observed. "I would much prefer to stay here than go back to New York."

"You're not American, are you?" Besserley asked.

"Her mother was an American," Mr. Homfret explained. "We have just been to New York on a visit. I am English on one side and Canadian on the other. Irish-Canadian, that is to say."

"I think you will need a little of the Irish optimism if you start with your scheme of selling bonds here, Mr. Homfret," Besserley warned him. "I have been thinking it over. I don't believe your scheme would be a great success."

Mr. Homfret seemed honestly disappointed. His face fell.

"I'm sorry you feel that way about it, General," he regretted.

"Well, I hope it comes off, anyway," Besserley said. "I am sure you and your daughter would be very welcome residents here. I hear the young lady's tennis is really good."

"It's not good enough for these people," she confessed. "I have lost both my sets to-day. There's my partner looking grumpy as usual. I don't suppose he will even speak to me. They say he hates being beaten."

Besserley looked round and raised his eyebrows in surprise.

"Well, he's not often beaten," he remarked. "If you were playing with George Brand, you were right up in the top circles."

The young man paused as he passed up the room. He smiled at the girl and exchanged a word or two with Besserley.

"Got over our defeat yet?" she asked.

"Got over it? I should say so," was the prompt reply. "I never played worse. Felt thoroughly ashamed of myself afterwards. I suppose you know, sir," he added, turning to Mr. Homfret, "that your daughter is a very fine player."

"I have been told that she is good," her father admitted.

"She's much better than good. We were playing against the best combination Monte Carlo can put up, and they only just beat us because I was out of

33

form. We'll have our revenge another time, I hope, Miss Homfret."

"And I was actually going to ask you to play with me," Besserley observed, as the young man passed on.

"Don't be silly," she begged. "I'll play with you any time you like — unless you are really bad, and I don't think you would be."

"Why not?"

She looked at him for a moment appraisingly.

"You don't seem to me the sort of person who would do things at all, if you did them badly. . . . Dad, could I have a few hundred francs for roulette?"

Mr. Homfret sighed. He felt for his pocket-book and handed across three notes.

"All I can spare, my dear, until after dinner."

"If I win," she promised as she rose and, with a smile at Besserley, prepared to depart, "I'll buy a bond."

"I like your daughter, Mr. Homfret," Besserley said, watching her retreating figure.

Mr. Homfret nodded a little absently.

"She is a good girl," he acknowledged. "A little out-spoken. I'm afraid you don't think much of my scheme, though?"

"I shouldn't put much money into it, if I were you," Besserley replied. "I think the banks here absorb what little inclination there is towards speculation, and I'm not quite sure that Domiloff would encourage his clients to put their winnings into stocks and shares."

"He seemed rather in favour of the scheme when I talked to him about it," Homfret observed.

His companion's eyes twinkled.

"Perhaps he doesn't take you seriously. You wait until some of his satellites come and tell him that the three or four thousand pounds the young man won the night before has gone into tobacco bonds, or something of that sort, that you have sold him, and the young man's gone home because he hasn't any more ready money! There would be the deuce to pay then, I can tell you."

"You really think so?" Mr. Homfret sighed. "Well, I don't know. I should like to try it, anyway. I wasn't thinking of going in for any particular expense," he went on a little wistfully. "I happen to have a fair number of bonds and some very sound shares and I could sell those and deliver them without having to go to the expense of an office."

Besserley stared at him for a moment through narrowed eyelids. There was a shadow of almost childish disappointment on the man's face.

"Well, we must mark you down a winner some day and see how you get on with him," he remarked not unkindly. "I must be getting on, Mr. Homfret. I won't say good-by. One is always meeting in this place."

He strolled off with a little nod of farewell. He met Domiloff stepping out of the lift and paused to have a few words with him.

"Your friend rather puzzles me," he observed. "He

and his daughter, too. Do you know anything about them?"

"Not I," Domiloff confessed. "I only know that the girl seems a well-mannered, straight little thing. A very good-looking woman she will be when she grows up. Homfret is quite a decent fellow, too."

"Has he been in any business or anything?" Besserley asked. "He talks about these bonds and shares in a very simple sort of way."

"I thought so, myself," Domiloff agreed. "If I knew him a little better I should be inclined to hint to him that the selling of these things outside a stockbroker's office is not a very popular profession just now. Shall I see you later? De Hochepierre's dinner to-night, you know."

Besserley shook his head.

"I'm going back home," he confided. "I mean to have a few days' quiet work, if I can."

Besserley spent the first two days of his absence from Monte Carlo in the fashion he loved. He rose early, swam in his pool, was massaged by a professional whom he kept upon his staff, took his *petit déjeuner* on the crazy pavement outside the Chalet, sipped his coffee and lit his cigarette in the warm spring sunshine and worked steadily until an hour before luncheon. Then he walked round the estate, inspected the growth of his vines, interested himself in the gardens and passed his judgment upon some doubtful timber in one of the higher plantations. He

lunched alone, also at the table outside the Chalet —
frugally but still in luxury. For half an hour afterwards, he dozed in the sunshine, then he worked for a
couple of hours, played squash with his secretary until
the light went, swam once more for a quarter of an
hour, changed for dinner and lingered over his wine,
watching the fading away of the landscape, the glimmering of the lights and the paling of the world as
the rim of the moon came up from behind the mountains. Afterwards, he dictated several letters, read the
French and English papers and a few chapters of a
popular novel and smoked his final pipe, strolling
about in the gardens where the night flowers had begun to unfold their petals. At half past ten he rang
for his servant and retired for the night, sleeping, as
usual, until well after dawn without a break. On
the third day, however, there came an unexpected
interruption. He was working exceedingly well that
morning when there was a knock at the door and
Henri presented himself. Besserley swung round
frowning.

"Against orders, Henri," he admonished him
sternly.

The butler extended his hands.

"But, Monsieur, it was difficult," he explained.
"Outside the gates, for most of the morning, a young
lady has been sketching. A short while ago she applied to the gatekeeper for permission to come a little
way into the grounds — the light had changed and
she wanted to finish her sketch from a different angle.

Naturally, the man refused. Mademoiselle wrote her name on a piece of drawing-paper and asked that it be brought to you. She said that she was an acquaintance."

Henri produced the paper. Besserley glanced at the name scrawled across the sheet in large but firm characters:

Mary Homfret

He nodded.

"She can come in," he told the man. "Tell Jean that he was quite right, but the young lady can be admitted. Do not disturb me again."

Henri disappeared. Besserley turned back to his work. Somehow or other, things did not go quite so smoothly. The second interruption was almost welcome. He heard a light step on the crazy pavement and turned his head to see the girl standing outside. He rose at once to his feet.

"May I come in?" she asked.

"Of course," he answered. "I meant to have come out and paid my respects before you left."

She entered the room, a portfolio under her arm.

"Sit down," Besserley invited. "Too early for tea, isn't it? Anything else you would like?"

"Not just now, thank you."

She leaned back in a corner of the divan. The pose might almost have been a studied one, for it displayed to their full advantage the delicate, shapely lines of her figure. Her hands were clasped behind her head. Her eyes travelled round the little room with interest.

"Father all right?" Besserley enquired.

"In excellent health, I believe," she answered. "Is this where you work?"

He nodded.

"I almost live here," he confided.

She was silent for a moment but he realized that she was looking steadily across at him with a faint smile upon her lips. It was a queer sort of smile but it did nothing to disturb the beauty of her mouth.

"Tennis going strong?"

She ignored his question.

"You can go on with your work, if you like," she said. "I am content to rest for a few minutes. I like this room."

He swung his chair round and looked at his half-finished sentence. Somehow or other, however, the thread of his thoughts seemed broken. He struggled with an idea and then discarded it. Presently, his meditations were interrupted by a slight sound. He turned round. The girl was leaning even farther back in her corner and she was laughing softly. It was quite a musical sound but somehow it disturbed him.

"You are funny," she murmured. "Come and sit here."

Her hand tapped the place by her side. Besserley looked at her with slightly upraised eyebrows. There was no answering smile upon his lips.

"Thank you," he said. "I prefer to remain where I am. When you are sufficiently rested to return to your work I shall be ready then to continue mine."

"Difficult," she sighed. "You are going to be difficult."

His voice became very quiet. An enemy of his had once said that the only time he was afraid of Besserley was when he whispered.

"Will you tell me why you have come here, young lady?" he asked.

"On business," she answered.

"Whose?"

"Father's business."

"I'm listening."

"He wants money."

"Money doesn't grow on this countryside," he told her.

"Well, Father wants some money very badly and we neither of us have any. We thought that you might like to buy my sketch."

"Where is it?"

"In the portfolio there — the top one."

He crossed the room, opened the portfolio and took out the sketch. He glanced at it for a moment. Then he returned to his place, tore it in half and dropped the pieces in the waste-paper basket. His action did not seem to disturb her in the least.

"You don't want to buy it?"

"No."

"Why not?"

"Because you haven't the faintest idea of sketching."

"You are very disappointing," she said. "Will you buy some of Father's bonds — just a hundred thousand francs' worth?"

"Certainly not," he replied. "Why should I?"

"They're quite good bonds."

"I should be inclined to doubt it."

She sighed.

"Really, you are very difficult," she repeated. "I don't think that the bonds are very good, though. The only man Father tried to sell some to wanted to have him sent to prison."

He looked away for fear she should notice the twitching of his lips.

"General Besserley," she began again.

"Well?"

"You are not very affectionate, are you?"

"Not very."

"I have just come from America," she sighed, "where things are so different. You don't even go to petting parties, I suppose?"

"If they really exist," he replied, "I cannot imagine a more loathsome form of entertainment."

"You wouldn't like to come and sit on the divan here and look into my eyes and tell me just what you thought about them?"

"I can tell you from here," he assured her, "that you have beautiful eyes. For the rest, I have a *valet de chambre* who has a great reputation for the sort of performances to which you seem to be dimly alluding. Shall I ring for him?"

41

Whenever, afterwards, Besserley, who throughout his whole life had avoided hurting animals, women or even anyone of his own sex, thought of that speech, he felt a curious but very humiliating sensation of shame. The girl made no reply. She sat quite still. So far as he could see, she was feeling nothing, resenting nothing. He turned round to his work and laboriously completed a sentence. When he looked round again she was still in her place but her hand was trembling slightly. Her eyes possessed no longer that gleam of laughter which certainly had had its own peculiar attraction. He almost fancied that there was a little quiver now, but a very different sort of quiver, at the corners of her lips. The very fact that he hated himself for his last remark hardened him for a moment. He turned back to his work. Very soon a faint sound disturbed him. Once more he swung his chair around. The divan was empty, although the portfolio still leaned against its side. He stepped across to the window. She was flying down the crazy pavement, running hard with the swift, effortless grace of a young Atalanta, running with her head thrown back and her hands beating the air. He called after her.

"Miss Homfret!"

There was no response. She was in the drive now.

"Mary!" he called at the top of his voice.

There was still no response. He watched her pass through the gate and jump into her little car. Soon there was a coughing, a wheezing and a spiral wreath of blue smoke. The car began to move. Down the steep hill it gathered speed rapidly.

"Hi — Miss Homfret!" he shouted. "Mary!"

The girl never turned her head.

Besserley found the incident, which a complete man of the world would have dismissed with a shrug of the shoulders, lingering in his mind all through the day, disturbing his pleasure in writing, interfering with the zest with which he plunged into the pool for his evening swim, spoiling the flavour of his cocktail, making him think for a moment that his pint bottle of Berncastler Doctor was corked. No one had ever accused him of being a sensitive man, yet he sometimes confessed, to his shame, that he was. He had the feeling of one who has set a heavy heel upon a beautiful butterfly. He woke the next morning with an unpleasant feeling that he had slipped from his place in life, that he had done something of which he was ashamed. Common sense came to his aid. Nevertheless, common sense brought him small consolation. It was another lovely morning when he sat down to his breakfast. The sun was shining with the same brilliance. The cypresses stood stark and still against an even bluer sky. More roses had blossomed since the early morning and the greater heat was carrying an even more delicious perfume from the cedar and pine trees on the westward side of the domain. None of these appeals to the senses seemed to bring their usual satisfaction. Even his after-breakfast pipe was uninspiring. He worked more or less steadily, however, until twelve o'clock, played three games of squash with a sort of bitter energy, took his swim and changed for luncheon, for which his appetite seemed strangely missing. His attempt at a slight doze was a failure. He returned grimly to his work. For once, he was relieved when there came a tap at the door and Henri presented himself.

"There has arrived a gentleman on foot who desires to speak to Monsieur," the servant confided. "His name is difficult and he has no card. It sounded like 'Omfret."

"Fetch him to me at once," Besserley ordered.

The man noted the tone of urgency in his master's voice and hurried away. He reappeared in a few minutes followed by the visitor.

"Monsieur 'Omfret," he announced and discreetly disappeared.

Mr. Homfret had lost his easy bearing and his neat appearance. His clothes were smothered with dust, his collar had wilted and the perspiration was dripping down his face. He sank into a chair without waiting for an invitation. The bag which he had been carrying slipped from his fingers.

"Where is my daughter?" he demanded.

Besserley wasted no words.

"Your daughter visited me yesterday afternoon," he said. "She stayed less than half an hour, and left at four o'clock to return to Monte Carlo."

Mr. Homfret's lips began to twitch. His blue eyes were very round indeed.

"That is not true!" he exclaimed. "She has not arrived at the hotel. She has not returned. I waited up all night. She is here."

"Don't be a fool, Mr. Homfret," Besserley said. "You can search for her wherever you like — the Château and this Chalet are at your disposition. I tell you that your daughter left in her car at about four o'clock yesterday afternoon."

"But her car — haven't you heard?"

"I have heard nothing."

"The car is at the bottom of the precipice on the road down. I saw a small crowd as I came up. They told me it was the car of a young lady who had been to the Château."

"My God!" Besserley exclaimed.

"There was a *garde-champêtre* standing in the road," Homfret went on. "He told me that the car was empty when it went over the side. He also told me that he met a young lady on foot walking towards the main road. That must have been Mary."

"I know nothing of her except that she left here in the car," Besserley declared. "I dare say I was a little annoyed with her. She wanted me to buy a worthless sketch for a hundred thousand francs, or if not, to promise to buy some of your bonds."

"Ah, good girl!" Mr. Homfret murmured, wiping the perspiration from his forehead. "I have them with me in this bag — the bonds —— "

"How did you get here from Monte Carlo?" Besserley asked.

"I walked all the way. I had no money. I had not even five francs. This is a very hilly place where you live," Mr. Homfret went on, dabbing his forehead again.

Besserley threw open the door of his very beautifully fitted-up bathroom.

"Go in and bathe your face," he enjoined. "I will order a drink for you."

The exhausted man, hugging his bag, disappeared. When he returned, he fell, with an exclamation of sheer joy, upon the large tumblerful of whisky and soda that stood upon the table. He set down the tumbler half-empty.

"Is this true that your daughter did not return to the hotel last night?" Besserley asked.

"I always speak the truth," was the dignified reply. "I sat up until between two and three o'clock, then I decided that she must be here. I had no money so I had to come on foot. I brought the bonds with me."

"Blast your bonds!" Besserley exclaimed angrily.

He rang the bell.

"Let me have the car here in two minutes, Henri," he ordered.

"I must find my daughter," Mr. Homfret said a little aimlessly. "If she is not here, where can she be?"

"How should I know? We are going to look for her."

Mr. Homfret finished his whisky and soda, picked

up his bag and followed his host a few minutes later to where a car stood waiting. They drove down the road to where the little crowd was still collected at the foot of the gorge. The *garde-champêtre*, who was standing in the road, obeying Besserley's summons saluted and hurried to the car.

"What about the young lady passenger?"

"Ah, I can explain that to Monsieur," the man declared. "On my bicycle I was turning the corner here when a young lady stopped me. She was English. She seemed in distress. She asked me if the autocars passed to Nice. I told her yes. One came at that moment. I helped her in."

"To Nice?" Besserley asked.

"To Nice," the man assented. "Then they came running for me, and I went to look at the car which lies below. It is in many pieces. A woodman told me that Mademoiselle stopped, leaving the engine of the car running, turned the steering wheel, gave a push and hurried off down the road."

Besserley expressed his thanks generously. They drove on to Nice.

"Some of these gold bonds —— " Mr. Homfret commenced hopefully.

"Hold your tongue," Besserley interrupted. "You can talk about your bonds when we find out what has become of your daughter."

With the help of a dozen detectives, eagerly placed at General Besserley's disposal by the *Chef de la*

47

Sûreté of Nice, they found her the next morning at about two o'clock. She was seated upon a stool smoking a cigarette at the bar of a night restaurant of indifferent repute. On the most distant stool from hers, an obvious gigolo was apparently sobbing to himself while he dabbed a towel into a bowl of water and bathed an inflamed eye. On one of the divans a young man was lying who was having first aid from one of the little cocottes of the place. Another man in a corner was eagerly talking to a sympathetic crowd at the top of his voice and continually pointing to the girl. At the sight of Besserley's entrance with Homfret, and the well-known faces of the detectives, there was an ominous hush. The proprietor, a small man with a black moustache, came hurrying forward.

"*Voilà la demoiselle* of whom you are in search, Monsieur," he said, pointing her out to Besserley. "When they telephoned me from the police I begged them to come and fetch her away. She has given what you call a black eye to our best gigolo, who merely invited her to dance. Well, perhaps he held her a little tightly. Another one of my guests she threw over her shoulder with one of those stage tricks. He lies there on the couch. Then Monsieur Rinaldi, an honoured client of the place, she slap him on the face and pushed him over — all because he asked her to dance! There she sits smoking quietly. One half bottle of wine she has had — no more. She spend nothing. She has upset the whole restaurant. People are afraid to go anywhere near her."

Besserley walked up to her side. She was wearing a

pair of blue trousers, a red blouse and a blue handkerchief around her neck. Her expression was exactly as it had been when she had left the Chalet, except that the curve of her mouth seemed to indicate a profound contempt for her surroundings and life in general.

"What are you doing here?" she demanded icily.

"I have come to offer you my humble apologies," Besserley told her.

Her eyes searched his face intently, almost passionately. She remained silent. Watching her, he became able to divine the torment which she had been suffering. Her breakdown, when it came, was complete. She drooped her head and then, as though suddenly conscious of her strange attire, she covered her face with both her hands. When she looked up, she was frankly sobbing, absolutely oblivious to the crowd by which they were surrounded.

"Take me out of this awful place," she begged. "I was mad!"

"You seem," he said kindly, as he helped her down from her stool, "to have been doing a little damage here."

"The men were rude to me," she confided. "No man has ever touched me in a familiar way. I cannot bear them to come near! Please take me away."

They passed through the door. The proprietor followed them outside.

"*Donnez-moi l'addition de Mademoiselle,*" Besserley demanded savagely.

"*L'addition, Monsieur, ce n'est rien. Qu'elle me fiche le camp. C'est tout ce que je demande!*"

Besserley handed him a note.

"Give that to the young dancing man with the black eye," he said, "and here's another for the waiters."

The patron bowed himself away.

"Where are your clothes, child?" Besserley asked. Her cheeks were scarlet.

"I was mad," she confessed. "When I arrived here I went to the G.F.S. The matron gave me a card to an old lady who let me a room. Here is her address."

She handed him a strip of paper. He passed it to the chauffeur.

"Do you mind going and changing your clothes?" he asked.

"No," she whispered.

The car came presently to a standstill. The chauffeur rang the bell for her and Besserley explained as much of the situation as was necessary to the porter's wife who let down the latch of the door. The girl was back again in ten minutes.

"I shall take you both to Monte Carlo," Besserley announced. "I am sorry I destroyed your sketch, Mary. I shall keep the pieces to remind me in future that I may suffer more myself if I ever lose my temper. I shall give you the hundred thousand francs for it, as a penance."

"Please don't be ridiculous —— " she began.

He drew her hand through his arm.

"There, my dear," he said kindly. "You see — a little caress. Now I have something to propose to you. I have a cousin, an elderly lady, who keeps a girls' school near Paris. She has begged me to send her, at once, a junior games mistress. After what I have heard of your tennis and seen of your exploits this evening, I think you would fill the post admirably. You will have to live in. The life is very strict but you will earn quite a nice little income."

She drew a long breath.

"Why, I have been applying for posts as games mistress everywhere," she confided, in a tone so low that it was almost inaudible.

"You have one," he told her. "It is settled. You will leave by the two-o'clock train for Paris this afternoon. When you get up you will find my housekeeper waiting for you at the hotel, say at eleven o'clock. She will bring you a letter to the principal of the school, she will bring you the money for your fare and you will find a little packet for yourself enclosed in the letter which will make your journey easy. When you have arrived at the school you must send me a telegram and I will write to you. Is that clear?"

"It is clear," she whispered.

Mr. Homfret stooped down and picked up his bag.

"You will not forget," he said, "this little matter of the bonds, General?"

The girl looked at him in horrified reproach.

"Father," she insisted, "be quiet, please. Those bonds," she went on, turning to Besserley, "are not only worthless: Some of them, I believe, are forgeries. My father was duped. He paid a great deal of money for them and he suddenly got the idea of coming down here and palming them off on someone else."

Mr. Homfret dropped the bag and covered his face with his hands.

"He has a brother in England, my uncle," Mary went on, "who would look after him if you would send him home. He is a clergyman up in Cumberland, and my father is quite happy when he is there. He was perfectly content with his fishing and his books until that horrible man came along and sold him those bonds."

"I will buy them from your father for five hundred pounds, if he promises to destroy them and return to Cumberland," Besserley proposed.

Mr. Homfret dried his eyes and opened the bag. The window was already let down. He commenced to tear them up until the road all the way to Monte Carlo looked as though a paper-chase had passed. When he had finished the last one he threw the bag out, too.

"This," he declared, "is the only happy moment I have had since that rascal came to the vicarage."

III

THE SMALL man with jet-black hair, pallid complexion and slightly hooked nose, — a figure of distinction whenever he allowed himself to be seen in public, — rose at once to his feet as Besserley was shown into the room. He held out both his hands.

"Ah, but my dear General," he exclaimed, welcoming him cordially, "this is indeed a pleasure! How many years is it, I wonder, since we met? Ten — fifteen — no, more than that, even. These meetings give a zest to life."

Besserley acknowledged his greeting with enthusiasm.

"It is a pleasure to me, too," he declared, "to be on familiar ground. I spent many hours in 'eighteen under this roof."

"Are we ever likely to forget it?" Gaston Lemprière said a little sadly. "Come, my dear friend, with me," he went on, linking his arm through his visitor's. "You two," he added, turning to the secretaries who had been seated on either side of him, "can continue with your labours. I am not to be disturbed."

The minister led Besserley into what was generally called the Holy of Holies — a small apartment, furnished with the utmost luxury yet with great simplicity, opening out from the bureau. He installed his visitor in an easy chair and pushed towards him cigars and cigarettes. He seated himself opposite. The room was perfectly ventilated, but it was almost sound-proof. The roar of Paris was only a faint echo in their ears.

"I asked a great deal of you, my friend," the minister said, as he lit his cigar and leaned back in his chair, "but I knew very well that you would respond. I brought you from your country home and dragged you into this maelstrom of noise and intrigue. What for? To ask you a great favour."

"You and I," Besserley reminded him, "have lived the life together which makes that not only possible but easy."

"Yes," Lemprière reflected, "we passed through wonderful days. You and I and Sir Phillip Osborne, the Englishman, and General Pelette — François Pelette. We have seen the colours upon the canvas of life glow and fade, loom in one place and disappear, blaze out in another and disappear again. May I take back your memory for twenty years and a few months to the time when you had passed into the secret service of your country and with myself and Phillip Osborne and Pelette representing the military dealt with many serious matters?"

"I am there," Besserley declared. "You need have no fear as to my memory. I destroyed my diary according to regulations, but there is very little that I forget."

"You remember at that time," the minister continued, removing the cigar from his mouth and looking at the ash, "you remember how perfect just for that portion of the year was the German espionage. You remember how we suffered, how we very nearly lost everything. Then two great coups came off. One was yours, one was Phillip Osborne's. France claimed no share in either, but I am not sure that these two were not the salvation of my country."

"They marked the beginning of easier times," Besserley admitted.

"One great danger still threatened us, one great mystery remained unsolved," the minister went on. "We learned a little but not enough. We checked the activities of the most dangerous spy who ever trod on French soil. As I say, we perhaps drew her fangs, but never has the greatest enemy France ever possessed been brought to judgment."

"My countrywoman," Besserley murmured.

"Sylvia Hume," the minister assented. "It was as Sylvia Hume that she spent her school-days at the convent in Paris. It was probably her real name."

"Has she ever been heard of since?" Besserley asked curiously. "I remember when we realized that she had disappeared. The lessening of the strain was tremendous."

"Yes, she is still alive," Lemprière answered. "She is as harmless as any woman could be. She might, nevertheless, bring about another war."

"I wonder what she looks like now," Besserley meditated.

"Would you like to see?" Lemprière asked.

"I should," his visitor confessed.

Lemprière moved towards a mahogany door on the farther side of the small apartment. He drew a bunch of keys from his pocket and unlocked it. There was another door behind, which he opened with another key. A formidable-looking safe stood revealed. Lemprière glanced at the calendar and made a calculation in his head. He leaned forward into the space before the safe. His fingers were busy for a moment. Then he turned the handle. A few seconds later he returned to his place with a picture in his hand.

"That was taken a fortnight ago," he confided. "On the other side of the quay there is a man who would willingly give a million francs for that picture. You are silent, my friend."

"I am bewildered," Besserley acknowledged. "This is indeed the picture of a beautiful woman, but except for the setting of the eyes there is nothing that reminds me of the vampire we used to spend our nights and days cursing."

"It is she," Lemprière assured him. "As I think you learned, Besserley, we do not make mistakes. With your permission I will return the picture."

Besserley handed it over and for the next few minutes Lemprière was busy replacing it, locking the safe and the concealing doors.

"I had two purposes in showing you that, Besserley," he said. "One was to gratify your curiosity and attack your incredulity. The other was simpler. It was so that you might recognize her when you meet."

"Is she concerned with this favour you have to ask me?"

"Yes."

Lemprière, even then, seemed in no hurry to continue. He gazed for a few minutes over the public gardens below and away into the blue distance.

"I must explain something to you, General," he said, "even if you fail altogether to grasp it. It is difficult for an American like yourself, with your standards and unity of purpose, to understand wholly a country like ours. I should advise you to accept the statement I make and leave it at that."

"I am content," Besserley agreed.

"France is a great country," Lemprière went on, "but in it there are two sorts of patriotism and two wholly different points of view. The one is the civil, the other the military. The real worship of France, the real soul of her patriotism, exists more in the soldier than in the civilian. Well, now I pass on. My own feelings, and I represent many millions of French people, towards that woman who did her best to wreck our country are dead. I have no desire for revenge. I have forgotten the harm she did. I am content to let her live. A soldier standing for as much, with regard to his country, as I do — a typical soldier, we might take Pelette for example — never forgives. He never ceases to think of his slain children, his broken armies, the peril in which his country once stood. If he met that woman he would tear her to pieces without a pang. If I met her I might pass by on the other side, but I would do her no harm. Civil France speaks like that. The soldier's spirit is Pelette's."

Besserley nodded. He waited for the explanation of the minister's words. It was not long coming.

"The military," he continued, "have no secret service like we have. It is our duty to work hand in hand with them and to take them into our councils in times of war or where any military matter is concerned, but they have no chain of informers as we have had working just the same ever since the signing of the Armistice, working actively now in every country of Europe. Sylvia Hume has become a lost soul to them. Our people have gone on and on until they tracked her down. We know where she is now. At any time we could have laid our hand upon her except for one fact. She has a great fear of us. She has never ventured into France. She has never ventured out of her adopted country."

"Germany?"

"Yes. She is on the point of doing so for the first time," Lemprière went on. "She is about to visit the Riviera. She has been advised by the doctors that her husband must spend the winter in a sunny climate. She is well-informed. She believes what is the truth — that the side of France which is dangerous to her has no idea of her existence. She may do right. She may not. She can come to the Riviera, for all we care. She can call herself, as she has a perfect right to, a woman close to royalty bearing a great name. We know that we should never touch her. Never should we give a

58

sign that we knew. But if Pelette's France discovers her identity it would be no affair of ours. It would be the military court before which she would be dragged. It would be the military who would send her to her death."

"And then?" Besserley asked, a little puzzled.

"Ah, my friend," Lemprière replied, "do not ask me too much. Be content with realizing this. Her name is written in letters of gold in the records of the patriots of the country for which she worked. She was their Joan of Arc, and they are a nation which does not forget."

"But surely, under its present administration, Germany would never dream of going to war for a woman's sake?" Besserley objected.

It was a question which so experienced a diplomatist should perhaps never have asked. Besserley himself realized that as soon as the words were spoken. Lemprière showed no concern, however. He shrugged his shoulders and treated the matter lightly.

"My dear friend," he said, "we do not need to go beyond what we can see. You would do the country which you have served a crowning service if you were able to persuade Sylvia Hume to recross the frontier. At a pinch, Italy would be safe. In that case the contents of this envelope would be useful to you. Italy is spoiling for war but she is not yet ready for it."

"I see," Besserley remarked, as he thrust the envelope into his pocket-book.

Lemprière laid down his extinct cigar. He glanced

at his watch and rose regretfully to his feet. Besserley followed suit.

"To talk of rewards to you," Lemprière said, passing his arm affectionately through his visitor's, "would be an absurdity. You have already received distinctions at our hands. There is little we have left to offer. Still, it is a great thing to have a country like France your debtor. One never knows. And there are those old ties, Besserley. One speaks of them so seldom but they are there."

The two men clasped hands. They walked together to the outer bureau. Lemprière himself rang for an orderly and accompanied his departing guest to the door.

"Never let it be so long again," were Lemprière's last words, "before you visit your old friends. Farewell, my dear Besserley. Success to these Memoirs I read about!"

The door was closed. Besserley had held his peace, but the minister was satisfied.

In the dining-car a few nights later Besserley looked with some apprehension at the crowds of people queueing up for places. His worst fears were soon realized. A tall man, leaning slightly upon a stick, had paused at his table and, after a casual glance at the reserved card on the chair opposite, was looking intently at its guardian.

"*Monsieur le Général!*"

Besserley glanced up quickly. For a moment the

60

stern grizzled face with its hard, clean-cut features, its somewhat prominent jaw, seemed strange to him. Then he suddenly recognized the speaker.

"Colonel Drousson!"

"*À votre service.*"

The newcomer pointed to the chair.

"It is permitted?"

"Of course," Besserley replied. "I was keeping it on chance for a friend. I never dreamed that I should encounter one of so long standing."

Colonel Drousson bowed slightly. He deposited his stick in the corner, hung up his hat and sat down.

"It is a great many years since we met, General."

"I am flattered that you recognized me," Besserley replied.

"I am not sure that I should have done," Drousson confided, "but yesterday, or was it the day before, I was passing the bureau of the *Chef de la Sûreté*, and I saw you come out. For a moment I was not sure, then later in the day I had a flash of inspiration. I knew that it was indeed you. Upon my word, it is a strange world this. You visit France often?"

"I have a villa in the South," Besserley told him. "I am on my way there now."

"Lucky man," Drousson sighed. "I am in search of sunshine myself. You retired some time ago, I think, from your military activities?"

"I changed them for a little mild diplomacy," Besserley explained. "I have represented Washington on one or two of these minor and singularly useless conferences. Now I have finished. I gamble a little, play tennis and golf a little and, like all elderly gentlemen, I am engaged in the futile task of writing my Memoirs."

"If you write the truth," Drousson observed dryly, "they should not be futile."

"Share a bottle of wine with me," Besserley invited, "to commemorate our meeting."

"I will do so with great pleasure," his companion assented. "Let our conversation be of the future."

Besserley smiled.

"I don't think you ever had much confidence in my gifts as a diplomat," he remarked. "Still, the dining-saloon of the *Train Bleu* would indeed be an obviously unfit place to exchange reminiscences. You are coming as a visitor to the South?"

Drousson's hard brown fingers played for a moment with his grey moustache.

"I take a few days' hard-earned holiday," he admitted. "I play roulette at Monte Carlo and a little baccarat at Cannes and I visit some old friends."

Dinner was presently served and eaten in some discomfort. The oscillation of the train increased. The opportunity for conversation became negligible. Besserley left his place before the arrival of coffee and with a nod and a word of cordial farewell to his travelling companion returned to his coupé.

"Drousson," he muttered to himself. "Waiting for me to ask him questions, too, the old fox!"

Besserley lit a cigar and concealed himself behind

a newspaper. Nevertheless, the closed door was presently pushed back. He lowered the paper to find Drousson leaning upon his stick.

"I finish my cigarette with you — yes?" he asked.

"With pleasure," Besserley replied. "I couldn't stand that infernal hubbub any longer."

"It is trying," Drousson admitted.

He knocked the ash from his cigarette and glanced towards the door as though to be sure that it was closed.

"My friend," he said, "this is a chance meeting, I have no doubt. It gives me an opportunity to say just a word to you which perhaps you will not take ill."

"Go right ahead," Besserley invited.

"You have retired, you tell me. You are wise. You are an American, you are rich, you are fond of pleasure. For me — I am a Frenchman, I am a patriot, I know no pleasures except one, that is — to serve my country."

"You have always done that."

"My memories of you, General," Drousson continued, "are curiously distinct. Considering your disposition, you were a shrewd and clever worker. But you had one fault. You were a little over-chivalrous."

"Yes?" Besserley murmured dubiously.

"The memory of that failing is with me, Besserley, when I venture to give you one word of warning. Ours is a great and powerful country because we do not brook defeat, because we never forgive and because if evil is done to us, though we wait for generations, we pay back the debt. My service, General, and I warn you that I have not retired, my service to which I still belong is ruthless. Nothing, neither friendship nor any of the gentler sentiments of life, enter into our consideration."

"Well?"

"It is just a word of warning, Besserley, that is all," Drousson repeated, reaching for his stick and drawing himself up to his feet. "You have retired, remember. You may pay visits of courtesy to our high officials, but remember that France is a military nation. She acts for herself as she thinks fit and she resents interference, even to the point of death."

Besserley sighed.

"The only change I can see in you, Drousson," he remarked, "is that you are becoming a little long-winded. Stay and have a cigar with me."

Drousson did not stay. He made no reply. He opened the door and closed it again after him with care. Besserley listened to the soft thud of his stick down the corridor. Then he buried himself once more in his newspaper.

Besserley, arriving in Monte Carlo in search of an Archduchess and one, too, returning to a life of pleasure after many years spent in the lonely forests of Austria, gazed for a few seconds almost in stupefaction at the woman who opened the door to him at the little Provençal farmhouse of which he had been in search, hidden away in a cleft of the mountains. She was still beautiful but in her expression was a great weariness. She had kept her figure, but it was wickedly concealed beneath the gown of a peasant. There was nowhere on her face the slightest signs of any cosmetic having been used to check the ravages of time. There were grey hairs, the spread of which could obviously have been checked, amongst the deep chestnut. Her eyes were still beautiful, but in their depths was a gleam of apprehension. She had opened the door grudgingly. Their eyes read one another's secret. She stood on one side for him to enter.

"Samuel Besserley," she murmured, and he would have known that soft liquid voice anywhere under any circumstances.

"Sylvia!"

They were in the great Provençal living-room. She sank into a chair.

"You startled me," she confessed.

Besserley, too, seated himself in one of those high-backed chairs. He remained speechless for another moment or two. All the time his eyes were absorbing her. It was she. Beyond a doubt, this was she. This was the terrible Sylvia who had cost France many divisions of her bravest soldiers, the Sylvia of whom Drousson was in bloodthirsty search.

"A few questions," he begged. "I have come here as your friend. It is necessary that we understand one another."

She made an obvious effort to compose herself.

"I am ready," she said.

"What made you leave Austria? Why have you come here?"

"I came for my husband's sake," she replied. "It seems to me that we have drawn into our beings all the damp and rain and water of Austria. We are ill for want of sunshine. The doctors told Frederick so. At last I could bear it no longer. It seemed to me that he was dying. I had to take him south. We arrived only last week. He is already stronger and better."

"And you?"

"What does it matter about me?" she demanded, she who had sacrificed a thousand men's lives without a gesture. "All that I want is for Frederick to recover."

"You knew your risk?" he asked her.

"I faced it. I counted upon being forgotten. Listen!"

"Well?"

"What are you going to do about me?"

"God knows!" he answered. "You have made it difficult."

"I made it difficult! I have made my peace with the soldiers of France. I am forgiven. It is you only, you and Lemprière, whose wolves of lawyers will tear me to pieces."

A moment before Besserley was confident that he was face to face with a difficult but a straightforward situation. Now, in these few seconds, he knew otherwise.

"Has Drousson been here before me?" he demanded.

66

She sat looking at him like a trapped animal. She was breathing quickly, and her eyes were filled with terror.

"Drousson," she repeated. "Who do you mean?"

"The lame man," Besserley replied. "The hunter of women — the killer."

She shivered.

"Drousson was never that."

"He was and is," Besserley told her. "I begin to understand. He has been here?"

"He has been here and gone," she admitted. "He will bring back my pardon and I shall buy a little villa and we shall live here and Frederick will recover — unless you interfere."

"In what way do you fear my interference?"

"There is the French Civil Government," she replied. "They have the elections always before them. If they spared the most dangerous spy who nearly wrecked France, what hope would they have?"

Besserley rose to his feet. He opened the door for a moment and stood looking out. The air was as strong as wine. He drew a long breath and turned back.

"Sylvia," he said, "you were never a fool."

"A fool!" She laughed bitterly. "Go on!"

"You are being fooled now. Drousson is deceiving you. France has forgotten. She wants prosperity and peace. It is the army who are bitter and unrepentant. They demand revenge. It is to bring that revenge that Drousson has left you."

"And you?" she asked. "Where do you come in?"

"I come from Lemprière himself," Besserley replied. "I came to save you. When do you expect Drousson back with that pardon, a pardon which, believe me, will be your death warrant?"

"To-day," she answered. "He promised. Then I go to buy clothes, then all will be different. I shall dare to show myself — the Archduchess of Fürstenberg, instead of the wife of a poor Styrian landowner. Sylvia Hume will be blotted out from the memory of man."

"If you wait for Drousson," he told her, "you will live just so long as it takes you to get to the first French fortress. Think — think of the past. Have you ever known Pelette spare man or woman? There is not a drop of mercy in his body. Not that you deserve it," he went on sternly. "You do not."

"Then why have you come to save me?" she asked.

"At least I come with the truth on my lips," he answered, "whereas Drousson's are steeped in lies. Lemprière hates you, so do the French people if they were reminded of you, just as those soldiers do, but Lemprière has had his warning. He is in diplomatic touch with Germany. The army is not. If they shot you the airships of Germany would be over Paris to-morrow. That is why I am here."

She sat down in her chair, covered her face with her hands and sobbed. Then there was the sound of the opening and closing of a door at the other end of the room. A thin, weary-looking man, still retaining, however, an air of great distinction, came quietly towards them. He spoke in German and he spoke quickly.

"Sylvia," he said, "I do not know your visitor but he speaks the truth. I have heard. Drousson is not to be trusted. All this time, every moment of the day since he was here, I have been afraid. I was mad to let you bring me here."

"What are we to do?" the woman begged.

"Have faith in me," Besserley adjured. "I have committed a great folly. I looked for you in different places. I expected the Archduchess. Drousson knew more than I did. He looked for Sylvia. You say he is expected back to-day. Well, I tell you that when he comes he will bring with him a warrant from the Commander-in-Chief of the French Army which no one here will dare to dispute. And that will be the end."

Her shriek rang out amongst the rafters. She checked it quickly and looked fearfully at her husband. He was shaking with emotion.

"You can escape that now," Besserley said, "but only if you act without hesitation. Come with me."

"Where to?" she faltered.

"Ask no questions, bring no luggage. Everything you require shall be found. The minutes count."

They obeyed. Besserley bundled them into the limousine and took his place by the chauffeur's side.

"The frontier, Paul," he directed. "Give way to nothing. Stop nowhere."

Paul was the best driver known on mountain roads. They were in La Turbie in half an hour. As they flashed by the corner they caught a glimpse of a car on its way up from Monte Carlo. A man stood up and waved his arm.

"Hold the road," Besserley enjoined. "Straight on — Menton — the frontier."

With all the ease of their eighty horse-power they swung round up the long ascent to the Vistaero and down. Besserley glanced once behind. So far as he could see they were unpursued.

"Stop at the French *douane*," he ordered.

The chauffeur nodded and obeyed. Besserley dissembled the spirit of haste which was throbbing through his whole body and stepped in leisurely fashion to the ground. He saluted the guard and strolled over quietly to where the sergeant was seated. He took a paper from his pocket.

"Monsieur," he announced, "I have here my friends the Archduke Frederick of Fürstenberg and the Archduchess. You observe that my name on the *laissez-passer* there is Besserley, General in the United States Army."

The sergeant saluted.

"*Mon général, à votre service.*"

"I bring my friends out for an excursion. Alas, I forget that passports may be necessary. I have travelled all my life diplomatically. The Archduke has never possessed one."

The sergeant indulged in another salute.

"We ask your permission to pass for an hour or so," Besserley said easily.

"It is granted, Monsieur," was the prompt reply.

Besserley went back to his place without a smile, and only a single word of thanks. He turned to Paul.

"Drive on."

He stole a look behind as they turned the corner. There was nothing in sight. They passed the Italian outpost. Again Besserley descended. This time he had even a better card to play.

"Your *chef*," he demanded. "Quickly."

The *carabinieri* hesitated for a moment but Besserley's appearance was convincing. He led him into a bureau. Besserley produced another document from his pocket-book.

"Monsieur," he said to the man in authority who was seated behind the desk, "here is my passport, which I seldom use as I have diplomatic rights. I am General Besserley of the United States Army."

The Italian officer saluted courteously. Besserley leaned a little farther over the desk.

"I have brought with me for a short excursion the Archduke Frederick of Fürstenberg and the Archduchess," he confided. "Here is their official permission to visit this country."

He handed over the document which Lemprière had given him. The officer glanced it through and returned it.

"Have you proof of their identity, *Monsieur le Général?*" he asked doubtfully.

"My word," Besserley replied. "Here, too, is the bag of the Archduchess. You will observe her coronet. You will observe the device of the great house from which she comes. I regret troubling you in this fashion but our excursion was not premeditated. We ask your permission to pass."

The man deliberated for a moment. He rose from his chair and walked out on to the pavement. Besserley opened the door of the car.

"*Altesse*," he announced in a tone of deep respect, "the officer in charge of the *douane* simply desires to be able to recognize you."

The Archduke was a sick man but he looked as much of an archduke as any person could hope to do in these days. The Italian was satisfied. He saluted the Archduke, he bowed to the lady, he waved to the road.

"Proceed, *Monsieur le Général*."

So they entered Italy. Behind them the pursuing car roared up the hill.

They dashed through Bordighera. They climbed again into the country of curving mountain roads. They reached Alassio. Besserley directed the chauffeur to the hotel, where he took a suite of rooms and ordered wine and coffee to be brought into the sitting-room.

"My friends," he announced, "this is where I leave you."

"Italy," Sylvia meditated. "Are we safe here?"

"You are not only safe," Besserley said, and now that the strain was over memory had come back to him, and there was a shade of sternness in his voice as he addressed her, "but the thoughtfulness of the *Chef de la Sûreté Générale* of France has made you doubly safe."

He handed her the official-looking paper which he had shown at the Italian *douane*.

THE ARCHDUKE FREDERICK OF FÜRSTENBERG AND THE ARCHDUCHESS ARE PERMITTED TO ENTER ITALY AND TO REMAIN THERE FOR SO LONG A PERIOD AS THEY DESIRE UP TO TWELVE MONTHS. THEY WILL BE ACCORDED, AFTER THAT TIME, RE-ENTRANCE TO AUSTRIA.

SIGNED, ————

ON BEHALF OF THE ITALIAN GOVERNMENT.

"I shall ask you," Besserley said, producing his pocket-book, "until you make your own arrangements, to permit me to become your official banker. These notes, Your Highness, will enable you to live without anxiety until you are able to reach your own resources. You will find the sun as warm here, Madame, and the people as gracious as anywhere in the world. I wish your husband restoration to health and for you, Madame —— "

"Not what I deserve," she interrupted.

"What you have the courage to wish for yourself," he concluded.

"What an extraordinary man!" the Archduke exclaimed as Besserley took his leave. "How long have you known him?"

"I knew him in Washington thirty years ago," she confided. "I played with him in his father's gardens."

The Archduke filled his glass.

"Let us drink to him, anyway!" he said.

IV

THE UNPREPOSSESSING DANSEUSE

THINGS were without a doubt going a little flat. The
Sporting Club supper-room at Monte Carlo was not
at its best. Cannes was entertaining that night. The
leader of the orchestra was away indisposed and the
music seemed to lack inspiration. By chance several of
the chief supporters of the place had engagements
elsewhere. Besserley, most sensitive of hosts, was the
first to perceive it. He cursed himself for the effect
those few hastily scribbled lines on a sheet of vilely
scented mauve note-paper had had upon him. It was
all so unreasonable — ridiculous. Yet, wherever he
looked that hideous sentence blazed out before his eyes.

*"You are in danger, great man. Something worse
than losing your life threatens you. It is disgrace
which hovers over your head — your honour which is
assailed."*

An anonymous letter but damnably, convincingly
phrased. The torture of it was spoiling his evening,
ruining him as a host. Once more he crushed down the
memory. He drained his glass and rose to his feet.

"My guests," he proposed with well-simulated
gaiety, "I think that we make a move. We will, if you
are agreeable, put our trousers on."

"What the mischief does our dear host mean?"
Michael Gunn, First Secretary at the American Embassy in Paris, demanded.

Baron Domiloff, too, rose to his feet.

"An admirable proposition," he declared. "It is a year since I was there. Our host means," he explained, turning to Gunn, "that we go down to the Knicker-bocker. It has a gaiety which I fear that sometimes this place, although I am responsible for it, lacks. In the old days when we came across a night like this it was sufficient to whisper 'trousers' and off we went."

They left the place, Besserley leading the way. It was one of his yearly all men's parties, a following on of his Armistice Dinner with a few of the original survivors for a backbone. They trooped down the hill, one or two of the younger members inviting a cautionary glance from the gendarmes and a good deal of mirth from the sitters-out at the Café de Paris by indulging in an eccentric dance of the moment. They followed their leader noisily into the small restaurant. *Vestiaires* swarmed around them, the young ladies quickly left off idle gossip or wasting their time with gigolos and took up their places at the "receipt of custom" — small round tables laid for two with a bottle of unopened champagne in an ice-pail. Frederick's reception of his guests was overwhelming.

"*Mais, Monsieur le Général,*" he exclaimed. "*Monsieur le Comte!* Ah, this is wonderful! It is magnificent! The round table — yes? We move everything in the corner there. Joseph is here with his violin to-night. Quick!"

Waiters were summoned. Joseph, lest there should be any doubt about his presence, came across the deserted dance floor playing softly one of Besserley's favourite airs.

"Three magnums of the Clicquot 'twenty-one," Besserley ordered after he had paid his usual tribute to the musician. "Everybody order what they want to eat. For me — bacon and eggs. This is the best place in Monte Carlo, my Parisian friends," he announced, "for bacon and eggs *à l'anglaise.* Joseph, I see you have your two tango performers here. They can give us an exhibition dance while we settle down. Afterwards ——— "

"Afterwards," Michael Gunn declared with a gleam of anticipatory pleasure in his eyes and pointing to each in turn with a courteous little gesture, "I am going to dance with every one of those eight young ladies."

"One at a time," his brother insisted. "Get on with the tango, Monsieur Joseph. There's a good-natured looking lady in the corner there with the sweetest smile I ever saw. I believe when I approach her that she will even dance with me. Get on with the tango quickly. I'll take a glass of wine while we wait."

Bland, an Englishman, had already deserted the table and was assisting in opening a bottle at one of the small tables, the young lady steadying his hand. The evening recommenced upon a gay note, the gaiety of which increased later on when, the tango dancers having performed and been warmly applauded, the little party of men took the floor. Frederick came

76

over to Besserley, a transfiguring smile upon his face.

"This is too wonderful!" he exclaimed. "For many nights we have longed for someone with spirit, for someone to come here and bring the joy of the old times with him. It is *Monsieur le Général* who can always do that. If I say little, sir, it is not that I am not grateful."

Besserley filled two glasses with wine, handed one to Frederick and raised the other.

"To the Knickerbocker — to Frederick — to Madame!"

Those who were dancing waved their hands and those who were sitting still raised their glasses. Soon the Knickerbocker was everything that a night club should be.

Everyone in the place was dancing. Besserley alone remained at his table, the sympathetic and happy host, notwithstanding the sense of depression against which he was always fighting. Then a girl came out from the retiring-room and took her place at the one vacant table reserved for the unattached young ladies. She looked round in amazement at the changed aspect of the room. Her eyes met Besserley's and she smiled. He rose at once and made his way towards her.

"I am the neglected host," he said with a bow. "Will Mademoiselle take pity on me?"

She flushed a little. Perhaps then Besserley noticed

for the first time that she was simply, almost shabbily dressed and that the arrangement of her hair lacked the coiffeur's touch. She hesitated.

"Monsieur is very kind," she replied. "I do not mind sitting out."

"But I do," Besserley assured her. "If you don't object to a partner who is a little out of practice."

"I myself am not very good," she confessed. "I have no right to be here, I think sometimes, with these other girls. They dance so well and I never seem to have the sense of it. Monsieur will excuse?"

They joined the gay throng upon the floor. Besserley, who was probably the best performer in the room, realized at once that his companion had spoken the truth. By degrees, however, she gained confidence. When the music stopped she was eager to continue. When he led her back to her table her eyes were bright with pleasure.

"I have never liked dancing so much," she confided. "You are very kind, Monsieur, and you dance wonderfully."

"You will permit me," Besserley said, "to order your supper. I always hate the look of those bottles and no plates. *Garçon!*"

A waiter hurried to do his bidding.

"Something cold, please," she begged.

"A *pâté de foie gras*," Besserley ordered, "and after that chicken and ham and a good salad. Take away this awful bottle," he went on, pointing to the ice-pail, "and bring a bottle of Clicquot or Pommery

78

straight from the cellar, vintage year — 'twenty-one if you have it!"

"You are being very kind," she protested. "The wine is too good for me. Please do not let me keep you now from your guests. It is not often," she concluded, "although Frederick is quite popular, that we have such pleasant company."

Besserley resumed his place and summoned the manager.

"Frederick," he said, "to-night is a gala. I don't know why, but it is a gala. You will serve supper to every one of those young ladies, you will remove those awful bottles from the ice-pails and serve them with the same wine as we are drinking, or something as good. Is that understood?"

"It is Monsieur of the old days!" Frederick sighed ecstatically.

"It is necessary," Besserley told him, "that every now and then we feel the pulse of life. We must not allow ourselves to grow old. I have just had a shiver. In the corner there is an enemy of mine."

"It seems scarcely possible that Monsieur should have an enemy in the world."

"He would kill me at sight if he could," Besserley went on, pushing away his plate and the supper with which he had been served. "I have known him for more years than I should like to count. He is a hard man, Frederick. I am going to drink a glass of wine with him and see if he responds. No, he will not look. Frederick, go across to that gentleman — the lame one — he is seated by himself. Say that *Monsieur le Général* Besserley would drink a glass of wine with him."

"*Parfaitement, Monsieur.*"

Frederick crossed the floor and whispered to the man whom Besserley had pointed out. He was a thin, wiry-looking person with haggard face, prominent jaw and deep-set eyes, a man who had preserved a certain military bearing but whose whole expression indicated a profound distaste with life. He received Besserley's message with stony indifference. Frederick, however, persisted. He became eloquent. In the end, with marked unwillingness, the man whom he was addressing rose to his feet, held up his glass and bowed to Besserley, who returned the salute. The gesture of the latter, however, was full of good nature and friendliness. The man whom Frederick had addressed as Colonel inclined his head, but there was a sardonic little movement of the lips which if it could be called a smile held nothing of either quality.

"Not much of a success, I am afraid," Besserley observed to his nearest neighbour as he resumed his seat. "I do not know why in life," he went on, "so many people like to carry with them their sense of antagonism, to nurse their dislikes and to stifle their better instincts."

"Depends how you were born and how you have lived," one of Besserley's old friends, an American who had a villa at Cannes, declared. "Some men's lives go smoothly from the start."

"It isn't only that," his host sighed.

The small hours of the morning were now established. Dancing became faster and more furious. Besserley glanced at his watch. He had one fixed rule of life which every one of his friends knew and to which every one of them cheerfully subscribed.

"My friends," he enjoined, "Gunn and Bland and all of you — keep it up. That is my advice. You are always kind to me. You will forgive an absent host. We are all friends. We meet every day or every week or every month so — no farewells."

"Jolly good move coming down here, sir," Gunn's younger brother declared. "Best place I have found for a long time."

"Glad to hear it," was the hearty rejoinder. "Hope you will all enjoy yourselves. Frederick, at half past twelve to-morrow morning in your little bar there you and I will meet, and if you fail to induce my friends here to drink another half-dozen magnums I shall be annoyed with you! You will have the bill ready — I will have the money ready to pay it. And so good night everybody!"

On the way out he paused for a moment at the table of his late dancing partner. She looked up almost shyly. Her plate was empty and she was drinking some coffee. Three parts of the wine remained.

"Thank you so much for my supper," she murmured. "I am afraid to think of how much I have eaten."

"You young ladies never take enough care of yourselves in that way," he told her in a tone of good-natured reproof.

"It is not always easy."

"Thank you for the dance," he concluded. "You will permit my little offering."

He held out his hand. He had crumpled up a note very small indeed, but she recognized its value.

"I cannot take that," she objected.

"But it is my pleasure to give it to you," he remonstrated.

"My dancing is worth nothing at all to anyone," she said, "and you on the other hand have learnt all that there is to be known about it — so you see I should have no excuse. If you would like to give me what the others generally get, that is, fifty or a hundred francs, I should be very happy."

"And I," he complained, "should be very miserable."

"Do you go about the world giving people happiness like this?" she asked a little abruptly.

"It is not often that happiness is so easily bought," he answered.

"Oh, but please, I take notice," she went on. "It is very seldom that anyone speaks to me. I am not pretty, you know; I dance badly and my clothes are not smart so I have a good deal of time to look round. I saw how you sent your offering to Joseph for the orchestra. I heard the orders that you gave. You have sent supper to all these girls here as well as to me.

It is a very wonderful life, yours, to be able to give so much pleasure."

"In a moment," Besserley declared, "you will make me blush. It is very little to do. This is a gala night for me. I came out to enjoy myself. I can only enjoy myself when I see happy faces around me."

"And yet," she said, dropping her voice a little, "you have an enemy in the room."

For a moment he looked surprised. Then he remembered.

"You are observant," he remarked. "You mean the lame gentleman of military appearance who looks as if his proper place were in a *morgue?* Yes, I am afraid you are right. I am afraid that gentleman doesn't appreciate me. To tell you the truth we have had a little affair together lately, and I think by chance I got just the better of him. He has not learnt the first lesson of life — to forget."

"He is not like you," she persisted. "He is a dangerous man. Was it in business that you met with success at his expense?"

"No, my dear, it was not business," Besserley told her, "unless you commercialize life and the passions of life. I saved a human being whom he wished to destroy. With his upbringing he was doing his duty. However, that is not a story I could tell you or anyone. Tell me your name."

"Yvonne Mauresque. If Monsieur could come again it would make me very happy to dance with him, but next time it must be," she went on with that little flush of colour again in her cheeks, "for what the other girls have."

He looked at her for a moment almost thoughtfully.

"Perhaps you give something," he said, "which the other girls don't. Good night. Any of my friends there are pleasant to dance with. Enjoy yourself and have as little as possible to do with the military-looking gentleman in the corner."

She rose from her place and dropped him a little curtsy. It was a gracious gesture even if it was not too gracefully performed. He responded with the bow of a cavalier and passed out to where Frederick was waiting to escort him to the street.

"Monsieur has done more than bestow upon the house a marvellous patronage," the *restaurateur* said gratefully. "He has given happiness to everyone. *Monsieur le Général* will excuse me if I make a remark?" he added as they loitered for a moment on the pavement.

"Go ahead, Frederick."

"Monsieur deliberately chose to dance with the plainest and least attractive of my professionals. Madame was pointing it out to me. If one has a heart one notices those things, Monsieur. It was a generous and kindly action."

"Look here," Besserley expostulated, "not too much of this, young fellow. If I did a good deed I was certainly rewarded. That little girl is unlike most of her class. She is still a human being."

"She has a wretched time," Frederick went on. "I have seen her night after night left alone when the others have all been dancing. She is always — the English word, I think, is — ladylike — so that no one could find any fault with her, but she makes no advances, she does not provoke. In her position she is useless."

For a moment Besserley hesitated. He had an unaccountable desire to ask one or two questions about this unprepossessing young woman. After all, what was the good? He patted Frederick on the shoulder, reminded him of their appointment in the morning, and made his way to the hotel.

At precisely twelve-thirty on the following morning General Besserley, debonair as usual, in grey tweed coat, flannel trousers and a Panama hat, with a cigar in his mouth and a bulging *portemonnaie* in his pocket, strolled down the hill and presented himself at the scene of the previous night's festivities. The restaurant was still in deshabille, but Frederick himself was waiting in the bar and Mrs. Frederick was making up the accounts. They greeted their distinguished client cordially and arranged an easy chair for him.

"My friends late last night?" Besserley asked as he accepted the bill.

"They left about four o'clock, sir. I think they all enjoyed themselves very much indeed."

"A nice bunch of fellows," Besserley commented.

"Six of them worked with me during the war. The Gunn boys I picked up afterwards."

"They are talking about giving you a return party next week, General."

"They are optimists, then," was the firm reply. "Not often I let myself go like that. Once a month is my limit. Do you find that right, Frederick?" Besserley wound up, counting some notes and laying them down with the bill upon the counter. "Now pour out that wine if you are sure it's cold enough. . . . Excellent," he went on a moment or two later as he set down his glass. "Best morning drink there is in the world. There's a little present there for Jules and a hundred francs for the *vestiaires*."

"Everything quite correct, sir," Frederick acknowledged. "The young ladies were all very grateful to you, General, especially the one you danced with. It isn't often that anyone takes any notice of her that way."

"I thought she was very well-behaved and agreeable," Besserley said. "Of course, I am old-fashioned, too. I rather prefer manners to appearance."

"She had another admirer later on," Frederick confided with a knowing smile.

"Capital!"

"The French officer, Colonel Drousson, who drank with you — not very pleasantly we thought, General. He came over and sat with her after you had left."

"The devil he did!" Besserley observed. "I

shouldn't have thought that sort of thing was in his line at all."

"He stayed with her an hour or more," Frederick continued. "In fact," he added, dropping his voice a little, "they left the place together."

Besserley was silent for a moment or two. Nothing in the world could have seemed more ridiculous to him than that he should feel any annoyance at that smile of Frederick's or that the fact of the girl's having made friends with Drousson should disturb him. Yet he knew quite well that he was displeased, and even the patron, watching that slight frown on his client's face, was not sure that he had been discreet. He banished the idea, however, as soon as it was conceived.

"Is she a native of this part of the country?" Besserley asked.

Frederick shook his head.

"I really am not sure, sir," he replied. "These girls come and go. They get engagements or try a change of dancing places. One really never has a chance to get to know much about them."

"She is quite one of the best-behaved young ladies who ever came here," Mrs. Frederick declared, glancing up from her book. "I wish the others were more like her."

The head waiter, who had come in a moment or two before to pay his respects, looked up from his task of unpacking a case of champagne.

"I think she came from round about Beaune, sir," he

87

confided. "I heard her tell someone once that her father was a wine-grower."

Besserley rose to his feet, straightened his already immaculate tie in the mirror and flicked a speck of cigar ash from his waistcoat.

"Well, keep your eye on her, Mrs. Frederick," he said. "Keep her out of trouble if you can. I shall now take my morning promenade on the terrace."

"And next week, perhaps, sir?" Frederick asked hopefully.

"I'm afraid," Besserley told him, "that you will have to wait a little longer for me. However, we'll see."

The terrace was crowded. Besserley found many acquaintances, the sun was warm, the breeze pleasant, the music delightful. Nevertheless, there seemed to be something not quite perfect about the morning. He was conscious more than ever of that wave of depression for which he was quite unable to account. It was not until later in the day when he found his thoughts wandering again that he realized a curious fact. He was not altogether pleased at the idea of Drousson with his stern eyes and hard, grim personality talking to the little girl with the wistful face. It was not at all like the large-hearted Besserley, but then, as he himself had more than once remarked, every man has his unexpected little spasms of sensitiveness.

He was to lose that indefinable disquietude within the next few days. Late in the afternoon he was making a rather half-hearted attempt at continuing his work in the Chalet of his Château amongst the hills when Henri announced a visitor.

"Monsieur will pardon me," he said. "I have been compelled to use my own judgment as you wished. A young person has arrived from Monte Carlo and desires a few words with you."

Besserley laid down his pen and swung round.

"A young woman?"

"*Oui, Monsieur.*"

His master hesitated. Already he felt sure as to the identity of this visitor, yet he hesitated. Henri continued.

"It is a young woman quietly dressed and of respectable appearance, sir," he confided. "She came by bus, I understand, and has climbed up the four kilometres from the road. I felt sure that you would not wish me to send her away although she declined to give her name."

"You can bring her in," Besserley instructed.

It was Yvonne, his little dancing partner. She entered very timidly, but there were signs of relief in her expression at Besserley's friendly greeting and the kindness of his tone.

"Sit down at once," he invited, pointing to a chair. "They tell me that you have walked up the hill — in those shoes, too," he added, with a glance at her dust-covered feet. "You must take some refreshment at once. Will you have wine or tea?"

"If I might have a little tea," she begged.

89

He gave the order and succeeded after a few minutes in setting her at her ease. The tea was brought. She helped herself with trembling fingers, but she was every moment becoming more composed.

"Do you smoke?" he asked, pushing some cigarettes towards her.

"I would rather not, thank you," she faltered. "I shall need all my breath for what I have to say."

"I am a good listener," he told her. "Tell me what has happened."

"After you left the Knickerbocker the night of your party," she began, "the man who drank with you so morosely came over and sat down at my table. He did not ask for permission. He just sat down. He asked me whether I knew you. I said that you had spoken to me only quite casually before that night. He seemed as though he did not believe me, but that does not matter. I told him what I thought about you and your kindness and he became angry. He told me that you were a man not to be trusted, a man with whom it would be dangerous for me, a good French girl as he hoped I was, to become associated. I had not wished to mention this to you but he had told me the same thing the only other time he had spoken to me. I was very angry and I would have asked him to go to another table but a thought came to me. I would listen to what he had to say. There was evil in his eyes when he spoke of you."

"Hates me like poison, I'm afraid," Besserley admitted. "All in the game, you know, young lady.

When I was younger we were mixed up together in some government business."

"He told me," she went on, "that you were the friend of spies, that you pretended to be a friend of France, but that you were working against her. It was then I stopped him. It didn't seem to me that he was going to tell me anything which it would be worth while for you to know and it made me so angry inside. It made me shiver everywhere to sit and hear him say unkind things of you whom I know to be so kind and generous. I asked him to go away as in my humble way I considered you my friend. He laughed, tossed a coin upon the table and left me. I gave the coin to a waiter and I followed soon afterwards."

"You left with him?" Besserley asked.

"It was ten minutes afterwards," she said, "but they were still trying to help him into a *petite voiture.* I think, perhaps, he had drunk too much. He called out to me and I, too, helped. Then he offered to drive me home. Perhaps it was foolish of me but he seemed so helpless that I felt safe. I agreed."

Besserley was a very human person. It suddenly occurred to him that he would enjoy a whisky and soda. He rang the bell.

"Take the young lady's tea away," he directed. "Bring a light cocktail which I will pour out for her presently and a whisky and soda for me."

"*Bien, Monsieur.*"

The girl continued her story a few minutes later.

"We arrived very soon at some flats. He told me

that his room was on the ground floor. There was no one about. I helped him across the hall and into his room. He offered quite politely that I sit down, but I refused. I was turning away when he pointed to a card which was on his mantelpiece. It seemed to be a card of invitation to a banquet.

" 'You see that, little one?' he called out to me. 'That is where this great generous man you seem to worship so will get what is coming to him! Bah! Good night, child.' "

"So that was the end of that," Besserley observed.

"That was the end until last night," she said. "I puzzled once or twice as to what he could have meant. I enquired at the hotel for you but you had left. It did not seem important enough to me to disturb you, but last night I was there at my table when he came in once more. Directly he saw me he stopped.

" 'Well, little one,' he greeted me, 'to-morrow night you may pray for your big generous man. He will be unhappy and he will need your prayers.'

"I did not invite him to sit down. I felt angry and I think he saw it. From his coat pocket he drew out the card which I had seen. He showed it to me.

" 'A great honour that,' he said. 'Perhaps! Oh, yes — perhaps!'

"He looked round for a table. I read quickly. It was an invitation to a formal gathering at some barracks to meet a very great man, I think he is the greatest man in the French army, and to take part in some function."

Besserley rose to his feet and showed her a square card which he picked up from his desk.

"Anything like that?" he asked.

"The same," she answered eagerly. "Exactly the same."

Besserley nodded. He was beginning to feel very curious.

"It is an invitation to meet a man at the barracks," he told her, "and to meet, as you say, a very great man indeed of the French army."

"And what does that mean?" she asked, pointing to a line at the top.

"That means that one is to wear all one's orders," he explained.

"I do not understand," she confessed. "It is strange."

Besserley, too, looked perplexed.

"Neither do I," he admitted. "He gave you the impression, though, that some evil was to happen to me for attending that banquet?"

"Please do not go," she begged. "I am sure of it."

A sudden light flashed in upon him. From his pocket-book he drew out the few scrawled lines which had brought their haunting sense of evil.

"It was you who sent me these!" he exclaimed.

The tears trickled in uneven fashion down her hollow cheeks, faintly stained with cosmetics. She answered him with a little choking sob.

"I dared not show myself at the Hôtel de Paris and ask for you. I wrote instead. It was after the first time he had spoken to me about you. Those are true words."

He smiled at her incredulously. The depression of the last few days had grown fainter.

"My child," he told her, "it is too great a *milieu* to harbour assassins. They could not poison me, they certainly could not shoot me. There is nothing in my life which could be so falsely represented as to merit the term disgrace, so you see your fears are groundless."

"Do not go to the banquet, please," she repeated doggedly.

Besserley was kindly but firm.

"It is not possible for me to stay away," he said.

"Please do not go," she persisted. "It is at the banquet that something evil will happen to you. Very nearly he told me and then he stopped."

Besserley rang the bell.

"Henri, the small automobile to take Mademoiselle to Monte Carlo," he ordered.

"*Parfait, Monsieur*. The box from the bank with your decorations and orders has arrived, sir. Are they to be laid out with your uniform to-night?"

"Certainly," was his master's reply. "I shall be leaving about nine."

"There is also," the man announced, indicating a parcel which lay on the salver he was carrying, "this box which arrived for you a few minutes ago. It is registered and stamped with Government seals."

Besserley took it into his hand and examined it

curiously. With a word of excuse to his visitor he broke the seals and opened the small wooden box. From it he drew out a morocco case and a letter. He read the letter, and although he was a man who seldom showed emotion the colour mounted to his forehead, his eyes flashed. He opened the morocco case almost reverently and looked at the small emblem in-inside. Then he carried them away and laid them upon his study table.

"Forgive me," he apologized to the girl. "What has arrived was unexpected."

"It is a joy for Monsieur," she asked timidly.

"It is a great happiness," he told her.

The servant left the room. The girl's lips were quivering.

"Please — please — please," she implored, "do not go!"

He passed his arm through hers and led her down to the lodge gates. All the time the words of persuasion streamed from her lips. He patted her hand tolerantly and assisted her into the car.

"My dear," he said, "you mean well and I thank you, but you ask an impossibility. . . ."

Nevertheless, Besserley was still haunted by the memory of the girl's eager pertinacity. He was in his bath before he thought of the solution. Then his shout for Henri nearly brought down the rafters.

Yvonne felt sad and anxious as she sat at her table that night. Towards eleven o'clock there came the thump of a rubber-shod stick close to her chair. She looked up in surprise. It was Drousson.

"You are not at the banquet?" she exclaimed.

He shook his head grimly.

"It was not for me, that banquet," he said. "I was given a card but my rank does not permit that I enter such a *milieu*. Shall I tell you about it, though?" he added with a satyrlike smile. "Shall I tell you what is happening there and why?"

She felt a cold shiver of fear. That diabolical grin was disfiguring Drousson's face. He was like a man revelling over some evil scene.

"I will tell you," he continued, slipping into the vacant chair. "Your great General Besserley, he has powerful friends in the Government of our country. There are rare times when the interests of the Government and the political interests clash with the military interests. Can you understand that?"

"Vaguely," she admitted.

He looked around suspiciously and drew his chair a little closer.

"Even I," he went on in a restrained whisper, "have to be careful. There arose a great question between the military chiefs and the Government. It concerned a famous spy whom with great reason the Chief of the Staff wished to bring to justice. For political considerations the Government seem to have preferred that she should go free. Whether your General Besserley was their ally or their tool makes no difference. He was the man who intervened, the man who saved Sylvia Hume from the firing-squad."

"It is like him," she murmured. "He is a great and generous man!"

"There are others," he told her with bitterness in his tone, "who think differently! Now I shall tell you the punishment which comes to your great man to-night. The banquet reaches a certain stage. Your General is there all ablaze with medals and decorations. He has been greatly honoured, that man. He wears for liaison services the highest medal bestowed by France upon an officer in a foreign army. He wears the medals which show him to have been present with the French staff during five of the greatest battles of the war. He wears a medal for personal valour rarely bestowed upon any foreigner who is merely attached to a French division. He tells his stories, he is bright and witty and then — a moment comes. The doors are locked. A word of command is given. Your General rises. Do you know what happens, little one?"

"What could happen?" she demanded. "How could anyone dare to do him harm?"

Drousson smiled with joyful malice.

"I will tell you," he said. "General Besserley is an American soldier. A French court martial could not try him for anything save an offence on the field, but a field-marshal is omnipotent. It is he who can bestow honour or take it away."

"I do not believe it," she faltered.

"Yet whether you believe or not," he went on, the malevolence shining out of his eyes, "this is what arrives! He is touched on the left shoulder, he is touched on the right shoulder. A corporal is on either side of him. The great man who is there barks out an order. Every decoration that France, the army of France, has bestowed upon that man is torn from his uniform. He is left there stripped of everything. Then the drums roll. He is marched to the door — dishonoured. He is marched out of the yard. His car is called for. The bugle sounds — just one note it is — a horrible note. He is gone. How do you think he feels just now, little one?"

"Oh, I think it is cruel," she sobbed. "Go away!"

"No, let him stay," a familiar voice said cheerfully from behind. "I should like to hear it all over again!"

Drousson fell back in his place. The girl sprang up with an exclamation of joy. Besserley sat down in the chair which Frederick was holding for him.

"So you didn't go!" she cried.

"You dared to accept an invitation from a field-marshal and remain away?" Drousson thundered.

"Let me explain," Besserley went on. "Within the last twenty-four hours I have been advised that the Order of the Grey Eagle, the most distinguished order which diplomatic France bestows, has been conferred upon me by the President. As I was on the point of dressing for the banquet the order arrived. You are a judge of these things, I am sure, my dear Drousson," Besserley concluded, pouring himself out a glass of wine. "You know quite well that the Grey Eagle could never be worn with military orders without special permission only to be obtained from a certain quarter. There was no time to apply for that permission. I was, therefore, obliged to excuse myself."

Drousson sat for a moment like one stupefied. Then he rose to his feet. He gripped at the table with one hand. He held his stick in the other. He leaned towards the girl with a threatening gesture.

"It was you who warned him!" he shouted.

Frederick had been watching. Besserley had no need even to hurry in his movements. Drousson was marched from the room.

There arrived an evening years afterwards when Yvonne was seated with her husband in their farmhouse kitchen after a long day's work and he found a faint, incomprehensible smile upon her lips.

"Tell me of what you think, little one?" he asked.

"I was thinking of a night I spent a few weeks before there came the letter with the announcement that my cousin had died in Madagascar leaving me that money which was just what we wanted for my dowry," she told him. "It was a night I spent then — the queer things that happened, Jean. A little word of warning I once spoke which saved a great man from humiliation and which brought to us, Jean, the money for my dowry. The other story was for the neighbours — that you know. Mine was just a little smile of gratitude that I had had the courage to speak out."

He passed his arm around her.

"For me," he said, "I smile when I think of the day when you first told me the story, when we handled the notes and bought this vineyard. Content, little one?"

"Happy," she answered.

Note. The name of the Order in this story is fictitious and the characters imaginary.

V

THE HUSBAND OF O-NAN-SEN

GENERAL BESSERLEY, half-way down the steep descent from the old town of Monaco, brought his car to a somewhat precipitate standstill. From the driving-seat he leaned forward and gazed across the moonlit waters towards the other side of the harbour. His motor yacht, the *Sea Spray*, swinging a little with the tide, showed the portholes on her starboard side, and Besserley fancied that he could distinguish a faint gleam of light from the saloon. He took off his driving-glasses and looked again more carefully. Without a doubt it was not, as he imagined might be possible, a reflection. It was a gleam of light. He slipped in his clutch and descended the hill thoughtfully. His captain, he remembered, was away for a week's vacation. There was only a boy on board as guardian. He turned to the chauffeur who had descended from his dicky and was standing at attention.

"Paul," he said, "is it my fancy or is that a light in the saloon?"

A mass of small clouds passed across the moon just at that moment and the lights of the port were more distinct.

"It is without a doubt, Monsieur, an illumination in the saloon," Paul decided.

Besserley glanced at his watch. It was already past ten o'clock.

"Only that cabin boy on board is there for this week?" he asked.

"So I understood, sir," the chauffeur replied. "Auguste and his brother are away for their winter holidays, and I understood that you had given Eugene the night off to go to Nice."

"That young rascal," Besserley observed, "has no right to go near the saloon on any pretext. I must look into this."

He drove on slowly, circled the port and glided past the line of yacht moorings on the starboard side of the entrance. Arrived at the gangway leading on to the *Sea Spray* he pulled up.

"Will you allow me to accompany you, sir?" Paul suggested. "There is a tough crowd around here at night sometimes."

His master shook his head.

"If I want you I'll call."

Besserley, in his evening shoes, made noiseless passage along the deck. He entered the bridge house, ascended two steps and with an abrupt motion of the wrist threw open the door leading to the saloon. His first glance showed him that he had nothing to fear. There was one person there only and he was seated before Besserley's desk, the contents of the drawers neatly arranged in little piles on either side of him. He himself, almost as though he had collapsed with sleep or with fatigue, was leaning forward, his folded arms clasped together, his head drooping downwards, his eyes closed. At the sound of the opening door he looked up. Besserley was staggered to realize that small though his body seemed, this was not the boy whom he had expected to find, but a full-grown man, an oriental with the jet-black hair and slanting eyes of the Japanese.

"What are you doing there?" Besserley asked sternly.

The man rose to his feet. His hands were crossed upon his chest. He bowed.

"I offer many apologies," he said humbly. "I may seem to you a thief who has entered. I am a thief but I search for one thing only and it has no value to anyone else in the world but to me."

"And why," Besserley asked, "did you think you would find this object, whatever it is, amongst my papers?"

"Honourable sir," was the quiet reply, "it is a long story."

"Stand quite still for a moment," Besserley enjoined.

The oriental obeyed. Besserley passed his fingers lightly over his person. Then he nodded.

"You are not armed, I see," he remarked.

"I carry no weapon," the man replied. "I left my bayonet in the stockades of Shanghai."

"What exactly does that mean?" Besserley demanded.

"I am a deserter from the army of my Celestial Master, the Emperor of Japan, a major by rank, and a deserter. The short space of time that is left for me to live I have employed in a search. So far, it has been fruitless."

Besserley looked with increasing surprise at the articles which were laid out upon the desk. The contents of the drawers had evidently been kept separate and each was arranged in a neat little pile. Even while Besserley was watching, the man commenced to replace them.

"What were you looking for?" Besserley demanded. "Money?"

"Oh no, sir," the Japanese declared. "I assure your Worshipful Self that I would not steal money. I deserted from the army, I have crossed the seas in search of a small box of sandalwood."

"Jewels, I suppose?"

The man shook his head wearily.

"Not jewels. A scrap of paper, just a line to direct me in my search."

"Your search for what? If it is not gold and it is not jewels, what is it that you seek?"

"O-Nan-Sen," was the tired answer. "My wife, sir."

Besserley opened a cupboard, produced two glasses, a bottle of whisky and some soda water.

"You talk like a European," he remarked. "Will you drink?"

The man's refusal was courteously expressed.

"I have drunk the whisky once before," he said. "Just now the Honourable Gentleman will excuse."

Besserley helped himself and sat in one of the fixed chairs drawn up to the saloon dining-table.

"Well, it seems you have taken all this trouble," he observed, "to be disappointed. Why do you expect to find this sandalwood box, with a lady inside apparently, in the drawers of my desk?"

The unexpected visitor from the East busied himself returning with meticulous care, to the various drawers from which he had taken them, the miscellaneous crowd of articles upon the desk.

"When war broke out," he began, "I was living in Shanghai happily married to her who alone has been the joy of my life — to O-Nan-Sen. We were young. We had neither seen nor felt any trouble. We took things gaily. At the sound of the first rifle shot I reported myself for service, as was my duty. O-Nan-Sen remained with her servant in my house in the Street of the Cedar Trees. Often I returned and spent time with her but soon we realized that this was not to be like the other little wars. This was to be the supreme struggle. We were surrounded by death on every side. Night and day the whole district where we lived was being ravaged. My regiment was ordered northwards after an attack which seemed as though it must lead to certain death. Then O-Nan-Sen lay for long in my arms, and when we parted she took the little box in which she kept the precious things I had given her and she showed me the place of hiding, and if her house fell about her ears, as seemed likely, if she were obliged to fly, she would leave the box in such place as appeared wise to her and inside she would write where she was to be found. There came a night when the whole quarter in which we had lived was razed to the ground. I had two days' respite while they filled up our broken ranks. I searched hour by hour. I neither ate nor drank. Then, in the ruined shop of an old curiosity dealer known to us both, I found not the box, but a note from O-Nan-Sen. 'I go westward with the missionaries,' she wrote. 'We escape. You will follow. I have taken the box. I will leave it in the small bazaar of Heratos in the town of Pening. Seek it again there.' Westward with the missionaries I understood. I rejoined my regiment, but after the next battle I stole out of the lines at night. I lay for many days hidden. I make my way to that town of Pening westwards. I searched until I found the small shop near the jewel market. The man who had kept it was dead — bombed to death the day before. It was his son who told me of the box. He had had it in his possession. He would have kept it, but they were in need of food. An Indian merchant hastening homewards in terror of the war had spent his last few hours in the shop. He had bought the box. He had taken it away with him. The boy remembered his name. It was Hussein, and he came from Port Said."

Besserley set down his tumbler.

"It is a strange story," he said quietly. "I bought a small sandalwood box from Hussein of Port Said a few months ago."

The Japanese inclined his head.

"I found my way to the warehouse of Hussein," he continued. "He remembered the box. 'It was nothing,' he said. He had sold it to an American gentleman in a motor yacht called the *Sea Spray*. I traced the *Sea Spray* to Monte Carlo. But now the time has come when all my money has left me. I am a beggar. I could not come as a purchaser. I came to steal the box."

Besserley refilled his glass. It had been a queer story, a story brimful of coincidences.

"You need worry yourself no longer about the money," he assured the intruder soothingly. "The box is yours."

The Japanese had been standing all this time. For a moment his knees seemed about to give way. They shook visibly. He clutched the side of the desk. Then he straightened himself. His eyes were glowing, his lips a little parted.

"The box — you will give me the box?"

"I will give you the box," Besserley promised, "but don't hope for too much, my friend. There is nothing there to speak to you of O-Nan-Sen. Behold!"

He drew from his pocket the little wooden receptacle in which he carried the two cigarettes which he always permitted himself before his evening cigar. One of them he had smoked that night, the other remained there. The box itself was the size of an ordinary small cigarette-case. Besserley had heard no sound of movement. Suddenly he found the Japanese kneeling on the floor beseeching him.

"Give me the box!" he begged.

Besserley passed it over. The long yellow fingers clasped it at first tenderly, stroked it, seemed almost to be talking to it, to be drawing out a speech of great eloquence, caressing words, sweet thoughts. They travelled — those fingers — over the back, they travelled round the front, they pressed and then, in the tiny receptacle which seemed to be left where a cigarette might have lain, the metal lining gave way and disclosed a small chasm. A strip of paper unrolled itself in the fingers. The Japanese stretched it out. His face shone. There were three words in Japanese which Besserley, too, understood.

O, my lover, come!

And underneath, there was another scrawled line.

Théatre de Bel Art, Nice

"To think that I carried that dozens of times," Besserley observed, "and to think — "

He realized that he was speaking to deaf ears. The Japanese sat like a man entranced.

"She is near here," he cried. "Théatre de Bel Art, Nice. Where is that?"

Besserley stroked his chin for a moment thoughtfully.

"It is a place where one amuses oneself," he confided. "It is close at hand."

"A theatre," the young man whispered. "I walk there — yes? It is far?"

"It is quite close," Besserley repeated, "but remember — what is your name?"

"Nikoli — the Major Nikoli. Nothing now, only Nikoli. I am debased."

"Anyhow, Nikoli," Besserley told him seriously, "it is not a very good place. Was your wife ever a singer or a dancer?"

"She sang ravishingly," the Japanese declared. "She danced like an angel. There was no geisha who could compare with her."

"Well, there she is, working, without a doubt, for her living," Besserley said kindly. "Any woman caught in such a catastrophe would have to do that."

The young man bowed to Besserley. He pointed to the desk.

"Honourable gentleman," he pleaded, "I have done my best to replace your belongings. I have taken nothing. You may search me if you will. I apologize — I beg your pardon for what I have done and I beg that you will let me go. When I think that O-Nan-Sen is here, I must go. There are passers-by in the streets who will direct me."

Besserley glanced at his watch. He reflected for a moment. Perhaps, on the whole, it was better that the wanderer should find O-Nan-Sen at the theatre than afterwards.

"I am a free man," he said. "I have been to a dinner party at which it is the custom to leave early. I will drive you in my automobile to Nice. I will accompany you to the theatre."

There was bliss in the young man's face. There was also hesitation.

"They will let me enter?" he asked. "I tell them that I am the husband of O-Nan-Sen."

Besserley laughed.

"Have no fear," he said. "I will pay for your admission, I will pay for the repast which you will presently, I hope, offer to your wife. I will pay for your stay, wherever you will, until you can make up your mind about your future."

The Japanese said nothing. He was trembling and wordless. Besserley finished his whisky and soda and led him up the gangway and to a place in the car by his side.

"We are going to Nice," he told the chauffeur.

"*Bien, Monsieur*," the man answered as he scrambled into the dicky.

The Théatre de Bel Art was even worse than Besserley had feared. It was a larger place than he had expected, with the usual auditorium, behind which was a sort of promenade where drinks were dispensed from two bars to the young ladies and their friends who sat about at one or another of the many tables. The roof was low, the tobacco smoke hung like a blue cloud over the heads of the audience. Nevertheless, the two late arrivals had one stroke of good fortune. There were two large boxes in the middle of the amphitheatre a long way from the stage. One of these Besserley was able to secure. Nikoli was still dumb. Occasionally he faltered a few words but his face was a shining lamp of happiness. Besserley was perturbed

110

but cheerful. He knew just enough of the oriental temperament to be able to hope for the best. The programme brought him rather a shock when he read that O-Nan-Sen, the most famous geisha from Japan, had been engaged at enormous cost to make her début in the Western world at the Théatre de Bel Art. There were pictures of a nearly nude young woman of the Japanese type with her limbs in most impossible positions ornamenting the cover. Nikoli saw none of these things. He brushed away the programme. He seemed steeped in some internal paroxysm which only revealed itself by the feminine softness of his eyes. He sat well back in the box and waited.

"She come soon?" he enquired once.

"We have arrived at the interval," Besserley told him. "Just half-time. The curtain should go up again in about ten minutes. Then there will be two turns before O-Nan-Sen —— "

"Her name is there in print — in print?" Nikoli asked breathlessly.

"It is here," Besserley acknowledged, retaining the programme. "She is going to perform, without a doubt. You will see her in about twenty minutes' time. You must pull yourself together, Nikoli. Afterwards I will talk with the manager. I will see how best you can approach O-Nan-Sen."

Nikoli murmured something about the god who looked after his father's bones opening wide the gates of Paradise to Besserley, but it was a speech which lacked coherence. His lips moved but his eyes might have been trying to bore holes in the curtain. The orchestra played a noisy succession of fragments. The audience filed in to take their places. The time arrived when the curtain rose. A young lady in tights tripped lightly into the centre of the stage, her left hand raised in salutation to the audience, her right to the man, also in spangled tights, who jumped to her side. The famous Hungarian gymnasts did their stunt. Besserley watched, a little bored. Nikoli watched with eyes that saw nothing. The turn concluded. The last spasm of applause was drawn from the audience. There was a few minutes' interval. The curtain rose again. A French comedian told risqué stories. Again there was a pause. Besserley looked away for a moment. He heard what sounded like a little hissing of indrawn breaths by his side. Nikoli was sitting there transformed. His eyes were fixed upon the stage but they seemed to see Paradise. The loge in which the two men were seated was a long way off and without a doubt O-Nan-Sen was good to look upon. Her dead-white make-up was effective, her white satin gown became her. The rims under the eyes were forgettable. Besserley joined in the general clapping. After all, he began to feel a little more light-hearted. It was possible that the evening could pass without tragedy. Silence followed the little burst of applause. Then O-Nan-Sen sang. She had not a great voice but her song was in Japanese and flowed very sweetly at times from her lips. Then she lifted her skirts not too far up and danced, danced to the curious birdlike chorus of her song. Besserley found courage to speak once more to his companion.

"Your wife is wonderful, Nikoli!" he said, as they clapped the conclusion of her performance. "No wonder she is famous. She has the air of being a little sad, though. How happy she will be to know you are here."

"She will be happy," Nikoli said softly, "and so shall I."

O-Nan-Sen sang another song and there was a ripple of interest when she slipped off her skirt and danced. There was a flame in Nikoli's eyes now, but it passed as he watched the grace of her movements, the soft finesse of the dance itself. He was trembling when the curtain finally went down and they rose to their feet.

"I go to seek her," Nikoli confided.

"Come with me, if you like," Besserley agreed, "but I think we had better find out from one of the managers here the best way to approach her."

They had no trouble. At the box-office they gained ample information. Mademoiselle O-Nan-Sen would appear in the promenade as soon as she had changed her costume. Visitors, even though relatives or husbands, were not permitted behind the scenes at any time, on any excuse. An attendant would show them the table where O-Nan-Sen would be seated. Nikoli looked blank and disappointed.

"You see," Besserley explained, "you are in the

113

West now, Nikoli. We do not do things so graciously as you do but then look at the audiences we have, and look at the money that is gained."

"It gives me no pleasure that my wife dances to please strangers and for money," Nikoli acknowledged sadly.

"Forget that," Besserley enjoined. "We have our little arrangements, you know. You will be able to take her away from here and start life again."

They made their way to the promenade. An attendant who was looking out for them, having already gauged Besserley's possibilities as a giver of *pourboires*, led them to a table in the middle of the space reserved for the service of refreshments.

"It is the table which the Japanese lady occupies," he announced. "She will be here in a quarter of an hour — perhaps sooner."

Besserley ordered a bottle of champagne and seated himself at the table. Nikoli was too excited to sit down. He walked up and down nervously, his eyes always fastened upon the door through which O-Nan-Sen would come. Besserley presently rose to his feet and joined him.

"My young friend," he said, "will you listen to words of wisdom from an older man?"

Nikoli's lips quivered.

"Graciously speak, sir," he begged.

"This is all strange to you," Besserley went on, "and believe me, although I am a Westerner, I know that it is ugly. It is not the place where you should

114

meet O-Nan-Sen, but to-night you will take her away, you will find your way back into the life you know and understand, and you will both be happy again. She, too, must have suffered; she, too, must have found it difficult to live."

"Sometimes," Nikoli replied, and this time his voice seemed firmer, "it is easier to die."

"That is part of your philosophy, of course," Besserley agreed, "but when one is young — well, it is not easy. To-night let us have all the joy of life. You and O-Nan-Sen are to be reunited."

Then he saw the ominous change in Nikoli's face and half-fearfully he looked in the same direction. There was coming towards them a girl hastily made up with patches of red upon her cheeks, the beauty of her mouth spoilt by an inartistic lipstick. She wore the tawdry confection of the Niçois over-flamboyant stores, her grace of movement had gone, her suppleness of carriage had changed to a sort of awkwardness. She saw nothing, as she drew nearer, of the shivering man by her table. She saw only Besserley — tall, handsome and opulent — smiling expectantly at her.

"You come sit at my table — yes?" she asked. "It is your wine?"

Besserley bowed gravely.

"But oh, O-Nan-Sen," he said, "there is something much more wonderful for you here. It is Nikoli who has travelled across the world to find you!"

She turned towards her husband and the pallor of her cheeks underneath that disfiguring rouge made her appear for the moment ghastly. Then she gave a little cry. She stepped back and then forward. She swayed on her feet. Besserley caught her just in time and placed her in one of the chairs.

"Talk to her in her own language," he insisted quickly. "Can't you see — the shock is too much for her?"

Nikoli spoke, bending closer and closer as the people pushed against them devouring them with eager, curious glances. Even to Besserley, his voice seemed full of the music and the pleasures of a different world. The girl's eyes never left his face, yet all the time she had the air of one struggling to retain her consciousness. There was fear behind the happiness in her eyes.

"The shock is a great one," Besserley said suddenly. "Nikoli, we take her away. Hold her other arm."

"I go away — yes!" she pleaded.

They took her outside. Besserley placed them both in his waiting car. She leaned back amongst the cushions and promptly fainted.

"Put your arms around her," Besserley told him. "The fresh air will bring her round."

They drove slowly along the curving promenade with the noise of the sea in their ears and the fragrance of the night wind streaming through the windows. Besserley listened intently and by and by he heard her voice. She was recovering. It was all the time more human. He drew up softly outside the door of the hotel where Paul had reserved rooms for them.

"You will find your apartments all ready for you and your wife, Nikoli," he said. "You will be best alone now. Take care of her and remember that she has had a terrible experience. Sometime to-morrow you can come or send to the Hôtel de Paris at Monte Carlo. I shall be there until the evening."

Nikoli helped O-Nan-Sen to descend. As she looked back she seemed to be struggling to find words with which to address Besserley. He waved his hand.

"To-morrow," he called out cheerfully. "We will all meet to-morrow."

He drove off, and although he was in perfect condition he felt the sweat on his forehead as he started back for Monte Carlo. The horror of the music hall, the sight of the girl for whom Nikoli had been waiting, pushing her way through the crowd of boldly staring men and lecherous women, seemed to have given him a sort of nausea with life. It was not until he had driven up on to the Middle Corniche and paused for a moment in a lonely spot that he could recover altogether his poise. He lingered there for some time with the cold wind blowing upon his heated face. Apart from that queer sense of defilement which was all the time troubling him, he had a depressing sensation of failure, even as he drove back through the sweetness of the night. He had tried to deal with a situation which was irretrievable. When he read the

117

few lines which were brought to his room the following morning, it was without any sense of shock.

Dear and Honourable Sir,

In a deep spirit of gratitude I send you the farewell of the stranger whom you have befriended. Late in life you showed me the vision of a new humanity. We die — O-Nan-Sen and I — with the pleasurable music of it in our ears.

The overturned boat was washed up on the beach late the next afternoon. The two bodies were recovered a week later. One or two lines recorded the incident in a local paper. It was not an unusual happening in those parts.

VI

THE TRIFLING LAPSE OF THE
MAYOR OF ST. MARAC

THE pedestrian, exhausted by his climb and parched with thirst, spent one of the most pleasant hours of his life seated on a wooden bench with his back to the stone wall of the Provençal farmhouse gazing across the smooth plateau over the valley, black with the pines which lined its gorges, away to the snowclad Alps behind. The air was a finer tonic than any champagne he had ever drunk in the luxury haunts below, the sunshine was better than any heat which had crept through his veins when sheltered by four walls from the elements, and the touch of mistral itself seemed to have all the excitement of the devil's wind without its cruelty.

"*Mais, c'est merveilleux ici, Madame!*" he exclaimed to the farmer's wife who handed him the jug of water which one of the children had fetched from the spring.

Madame smiled with tolerant courtesy.

"It is the same for us always," she said. "*Monsieur a fait une bonne promenade?*"

"Lost my way," Besserley confessed. "I'm thankful that I did. Is this your daughter?" he added, looking up as a girl, accompanied by a young man, came round the corner of the building.

"My eldest," Madame confided.

"And her fiancé?"

The woman sighed.

"It is difficult to say," she admitted. "He is a good lad, but they earn so little at that age. Still, it will probably arrive, that. Antoinette, here is a gentleman who has lost his way."

The girl smiled her greeting. The young man touched his forehead respectfully.

"Your mother is saving my life," Besserley declared. "You are very fortunate to live in such a beautiful spot."

"One is never weary of the mountains," she said, "but I like it also where Georges here lives — halfway down in the valley."

"Perhaps you may try a change of air some day," he suggested smiling.

The girl touched her companion's arm affectionately.

"We hope so," she murmured half under her breath.

They passed on, leaving Besserley to his alfresco luncheon. He ate the coarse bread of the country, goat's milk cheese and lettuce, and he drank from his silver flask whisky diluted with water which had come tumbling down from the snows. Madame sometimes appeared in the doorway which led into the stone-floored living-room to offer a cheery word of encouragement. Antoinette, too, returned to offer him another jug of water. Sometimes rosy-faced children peeped at him from round the corner. Once Monsieur himself, who was toiling in a small patch of oats, came to the house for a drink and pulled off his cap in greeting to the stranger. It was all very pastoral and pleasant.

Besserley stretched out his limbs and lit his pipe with a sense of complete content. Never before, he thought, had he presented such a disreputable figure to the world, for his foot had slipped more than once in the dangerous places below the pine woods, his khaki shorts were torn, his shoes bespattered with mud and dust, his shirt was open at the throat, his neck-tie in his pocket. He laughed softly as he contemplated himself. He, a man noted for the precision of his toilet, had become first cousin to a scarecrow. He watched the leaning of the sun and rose at last unwillingly to his feet. He held a hundred-franc note crumpled up in his hand.

"Madame!" he called.

Madame appeared, wiping her hands upon her apron, herself glad, it seemed, of the brief respite from her labour of bread-making.

"Monsieur?"

"I offer you my best thanks," Besserley said, "for your delicious repast. It is long since I have enjoyed such excellent food in such wonderful surroundings."

"Monsieur is very welcome," the woman assured him.

"You have so many things here," he went on. "I see you have your little patch of grain, your pasturage, your fig and apple trees and even your vegetables. A flower garden you can never need," he added, looking around at the wild orchids and harebells swinging a little in the breeze, the yellow marigolds and the cuckoo flowers.

"It is very wonderful here," she admitted, "and the air for the children, it is marvellous. They speak of a hotel, though, and a road before long. August, my husband, and I pray that it may never happen in our time."

"I join my prayers with yours, Madame," Besserley said. "Your husband spoke, I believe, of a foot-path to La Turbie."

"It is there, Monsieur," the woman pointed out, indicating a narrow rocky way at the edge of the plateau. "Monsieur descends for a while but it is always easy to find."

Besserley held out his hand. She drew back with a little smile.

"Monsieur will excuse?" she begged. "He is very welcome to the little he has had."

"But, Madame," Besserley expostulated, "you will permit a small offering like this for the children. It will give me so much pleasure if you will be so gracious."

She shook her head.

"My husband would never forgive me, sir," she said simply. "I wish you a pleasant walk home."

She threw him a little smile of farewell. Besserley turned away with one of his most courtierlike bows. She had supplied the one note of kindly humanity which completed the perfect morning.

It was many months afterwards when Besserley once more climbed on to the plateau and even then, though his car waited below and the route had been only moderately rough, he paused for a moment to fan himself. He was almost immediately conscious of a sense of disappointment. There were warning notes to spoil the tranquil and serene beauty of the scene which had never wholly left his memory. A black-and-white surveyor's pole stood at one edge of the plateau. There were others farther afield. A yard or so of that virgin and exquisite turf had been cut up. A disagreeable-looking youth was peering through an instrument. Several older men were bending over a plan. Besserley passed them all with a courteous good morning and approached the farmhouse. He stood on the threshold and looked into the stone-flagged living-room. The woman was seated there at the table, her elbows resting upon its edge, her face supported in her hands. It seemed to the intruder sacrilegious not to ignore the agony in her expression.

"Madame," he greeted her, "it is your hungry traveller — in better state this time, I am glad to say — who has returned to bid you *bonjour*."

The woman rose at once to her feet. After that first attempt at a smile, however, she kept her face a little turned away.

"This time," Besserley continued, "I do not come to beg for your hospitality, Madame. I have not lost my sandwiches. I have ridden nearly all the way here in a well-sprung car. The parcel under my arm is nothing but chocolates for your children, which I beg you will give them presently. Your husband is well, I hope?"

"My husband is well, sir, I thank you," she replied. "He is at work somewhere on the farm."

"You permit that I rest for a moment?" he asked.

She brushed the seat of one of the old-fashioned chairs with a duster and placed it for him near the window.

"Willingly, Monsieur."

Besserley sat down and looked at the mantelpiece.

"I see that your husband smokes," he said. "You will permit that I fill my pipe?"

She bowed her head silently. The life had gone out of the woman. She seemed almost to have become physically shrunken.

"Now, if it is not impertinent of a stranger," he went on, "will you tell me what these men are doing outside?"

"We do not altogether understand, Monsieur," the woman replied, "but they have been giving us sad news. They say that this place does not belong to us any longer, that soon we shall have our notice to leave it, that they are going to build a hotel here. It is the only home we have, Monsieur. We are both very distressed."

"May I ask you a few questions?" Besserley begged, "as a well-wisher, you will understand, Madame, with no desire to seem curious."

"Ask anything you will, sir," she assented. "An educated gentleman like you might perhaps be helpful. August spoke of going to-morrow to see an *avocat* at Nice."

"Then tell me this," he began. "How was it you thought that this place belonged to you?"

She moved to a great cupboard, opened the door and brought out a box. From the box she drew a sheet of rough parchment.

"All the land here has run wild for generations," she said. "My grandfather built this farmhouse with his own hands from the stone which they brought up from the valley there. He lived here all his life; so did my father and mother. I was born here. Soon after my father died the mayor of St. Marac came to see us and told us that this land was part of the *Commune*. We did not complain, but in the end we gave every *sou* we had saved to a notary and he gave us a paper signed by the mayor which I thought made the place ours forever. August, who is a better scholar than I, though, says that it is only a lease."

"May I read it?" her listener begged.

She placed the document in his hands. Besserley read it with some difficulty, for the French was curious and some of the phrases were obviously patois.

"This appears to me to be a lease," he admitted; "a lease, too, for ninety-nine years, which is certainly all that you would require. It guarantees you occupation, in return for which you are to pay a yearly rent of five *mille*."

"Five *mille!* Neither my husband nor I knew anything of that, sir," the woman exclaimed.

"You have paid nothing?"

"Nothing," she answered. "We have never been asked for a *sou*. What we have saved we have spent on manure for the fields, planting new fruit trees, buying a little more stock."

"Now tell me, who is this man who signed the deed? His name seems to be Forniquot."

"That was the mayor of St. Marac in those days," she confided. "He is dead. It is his son who is mayor to-day. His name, too, is Pierre Forniquot and he lives at St. Marac."

"Has he ever visited you — do you know him?" Besserley asked.

"He has been here often lately," the woman replied. "He looks at my daughter Antoinette, but that would make me very unhappy. We do not like him. Neither does Antoinette. He has a wild reputation in the valley. When he comes he always asks for a document we hold. I do not trust him, so I always say that I cannot find it. He had tried hard to get it from me or from August but we shake our heads. We say that we know nothing. Then suddenly — you see what has arrived — all these men who mock at us and say they are going to pull down our farmhouse! They say they are working for a syndicate of men and it is Monsieur Pierre Forniquot who has sent them here. We have had letters," the woman went on, "but it is very terrible that neither my husband nor I can read."

"Might I see the letters?"

She produced them. One was without a doubt a notice of eviction. Another gave notice that the property was now transferred to a company of which Pierre Forniquot was president. Besserley folded them up.

"This is quite a serious matter, Madame," he said gravely.

She turned on him wildly.

"Monsieur," she cried, "you call it serious? What is it to me who was born here, who have lived here all my life, who have toiled and sweated with my husband and my children to keep the farm going, to add to it little by little so that we may have a home for our old age? What do you think it means to us, Monsieur? Where do we go? There is nowhere. We do not own even a cowshed. We have no place in the world if we are forced to leave here, and that brute, that villain Pierre Forniquot leers at my daughter and says that we must find friends and work elsewhere! He dares to say that he will find Antoinette a place."

"Will you trust me with that other document as well as with these letters?" Besserley asked. "I promise you that I shall make no use of them except to try and help you."

The woman handed him the paper.

"I do not know who you are, sir," she told him, "but I would trust anything you said. If you can help, there are nine children and my husband and I, and if you can save us from this terrible thing there

is not one of us who will not be on our knees every
night to thank God for sending you here."

"I am not a lawyer," Besserley warned her, "and of
course there will be difficulties. All the same, I will
see, Madame, what can be done. Mind you," he said,
taking her hand and holding it kindly, "I make no
promises, Madame, but I feel strongly about this business. I will do what I can. You for your part must do
this. Keep your husband from worrying, keep him
from doing anything rash —— "

"Ah, the poor man," she interrupted. "I know what
you mean! He has spoken of it. He thinks if the worst
comes and we are driven out we shall be better without
him. Anything rather than that, Monsieur."

"I should think so," Besserley agreed. "And look
after your daughter, Madame. Don't let her have any
foolish ideas of self-sacrifice. Not until I have found
out what can be done."

"You will come again?" she begged.

"Of course I shall come again," he promised her.
"Within three days. Keep smiling, Madame. Laugh
it off with your husband. Tell him you have found a
friend. Take no notice of these disturbing ghouls. We
should never allow ourselves to be terrified, remember," he added, picking up his hat, "by the ghosts of
things which may happen. The foundation stone of
that hotel is not yet laid."

It had been in Besserley's mind to have played a
round of golf at Mont Agel on his way back, but he

abandoned the idea. When he climbed into his car he gave the chauffeur another address.

The critical moment in the lives of Monsieur August Dubler, Madame Dubler, Mademoiselle Antoinette Dubler and eight other young persons of various ages constituting the whole family, really took place in the bank manager's office at Monte Carlo three days later. The bank manager was evidently in a state of indecision. He leaned back in his chair and studied the little pile of notes tantalizingly arranged upon his blotting-paper. He looked also at the form of receipt which Maître Nessyen, the *avocat*, had spread out before him. Besserley, for whom Nessyen was acting, remained in the background.

"You see, Mr. Phillipson," the *avocat* pointed out. "I am asking you to do nothing in the least unusual, in fact I am asking you for something which I think you would find it very difficult to refuse. The agreement distinctly says that this man August Dubler is to have the enjoyment of the land he is at present occupying, and the buildings which his wife's father and grandfather erected upon it, for a period of ninety-nine years, which, of course, is a legal absurdity but certainly conveys the right to Dubler to occupy those premises undisturbed during his lifetime."

"So far as that is concerned," the bank manager agreed, "I quite follow you but —— "

"One moment, please, Mr. Phillipson," Nessyen interrupted. "The only stipulation is that our friend, the tenant, should pay a rent of five *mille* annually, which, as a matter of fact, is a very considerable rental to ask for mountain land. Now, Monsieur Dubler has been in possession of that land since the seventeenth of October, nineteen-twenty. The rent, therefore, till next October the seventeenth, works out at ninety thousand francs. Then, the rent not having been applied for, comes the question of interest. Here my client is acting with the most amazing generosity. No one is supposed to pay, in this country, for anything until he is asked for it. Nevertheless, my client has added to that sum interest at the rate of five per cent. The money lies before you, Mr. Phillipson, and all that we are asking you to do is to sign a receipt for that sum on account of Monsieur Pierre Forniquot, the son of the Pierre Forniquot whose signature is there. A receipt, remember, commits you to nothing except to a statement of the fact that you have received the money."

Mr. Phillipson took up the pen. He still had that half-uneasy feeling that he ought perhaps to refer the matter to his very much disliked and unpopular client, Monsieur Pierre Forniquot, before he gave the receipt. On the other hand he could scarcely be blamed for acceding to the request of these two important and influential gentlemen who, for some reason of their own, wished this matter dealt with at once. The money was there. It was to be paid into the account of Pierre

Forniquot. The bank manager, with a little sigh of resignation, scrawled his name on the desired line and rang the bell. To the clerk who answered it he handed over the money.

"This is to be credited to the account of Monsieur Pierre Forniquot of St. Marac," he instructed. "See that he receives an advice this morning of the payment made by Maître Nessyen on account of Monsieur August Dubler."

The bank clerk took the money without emotion and left the room. It was not for him to show any elation at the fact that the sum he held in his hand could liquidate the most doubtful overdraft they had on their books.

"I have done as you asked," the bank manager declared, turning to Nessyen, "especially since you tell us that our very valued client and friend, General Besserley, is interested in the matter, but frankly there seems to be something a little mysterious about it. There are rumours that a company has been formed to build a big hotel on the site of the farm. I do not know where it is, even," he went on. "It is too high up in the clouds for me."

"It is a pretty good climb from my Château," Besserley reflected. "I walked it once and I was never hotter in my life. Still," he added, rising to his feet, "it was an excursion I don't regret."

Monsieur Pierre Forniquot was, in his own opinion, a very fine fellow; in the eyes of the young girls of

St. Marac, who would willingly have exchanged their unmarried state for the high honour of becoming mayoress of St. Marac, just a little of a coxcomb, and in the opinion of the rest of the world a conceited young ass. On that particular morning it had given him pleasure to attire himself in the showiest-looking clothes he possessed. In the checked plus-fours, reaching almost to his ankles, which he fondly believed were the last word in English sporting habiliments, a shirt and a tie aflame with colour, black and white shoes and a green Homburg hat, he drove his small Citroën from the pleasant valley in which was situated the old town of St. Marac up into the mountain solitudes where several people of local distinction, including an architect, were awaiting him. Ignorant of the fact that either he or the *Commune* of St. Marac was at that moment to be enriched to the tune of something well over one hundred thousand francs, he assumed, nevertheless, all the airs of a financier of importance as he conversed with the architect.

"If you are fortunate enough," he told him, "to produce a plan of which my committee approves, there are just one or two things I should like to impress upon you."

"There is a good deal of information I shall require," the architect pointed out, "before I am in a position to start making a plan. For one thing I want to survey the actual terrain, then I shall require to know exactly the available capital."

The young man glanced towards the farmhouse.

"In that case," he said, "perhaps Monsieur De-troyat here or one of the others will just show you the exact boundaries of the site while I speak to the farmer."

He strolled away, taking care not to hear the ir-ritated remonstrances of the men who had been a long time awaiting his coming. The door of the farmhouse was closed but without troubling himself to go to the ceremony of knocking, he raised the latch and entered. It was scarcely a happy-looking interior. Madame was seated at the end of the table, her arms folded, her head downcast in an attitude of dejection. Her husband, a fine fellow still, but with something of the weariness of the overworked and underfed peasant in lonely districts, was standing gloomily upon the boundary of the huge chimney-place. Antoinette, at that moment strangely pale notwithstanding her out-of-door life, was seated at the table, a reflection of the family trouble clearly visible in her woebegone ex-pression. There were other children in evidence — the two youngest sprawling on the hearthrug. The young man looked about him with an air of distaste. He had, however, the demeanour of one who is about to dispel the unhappiness everywhere visible.

"*Madame et Monsieur Dubler*," he said, "and you, my little Antoinette, I am glad to find you all to-gether. I hope before I leave to see you all looking a great deal more cheerful. I have come on a special affair."

They were all listening to him but there was nothing

yet of that joyous expectancy in their faces which he had anticipated. It was Madame who spoke.

"Have you come to tell us that it is finished with, this wicked scheme of destroying our home?" she asked bluntly.

"The building of the hotel," he replied evasively, "will indirectly bring a fortune to the district. My mission, however, is more personal. I come to present myself as a suitor for Antoinette in marriage."

There was complete silence. Forniquot looked from one to the other with the air of one who fails to understand.

"It is clear, that which I said?" he asked. "It will be a great event for Antoinette. We will be married in St. Marac. It is many years since a mayor of the place was married from the *Mairie*. She can begin to collect her trousseau. I shall be ready in two months. That will make you happy, little one?" he went on, strolling over and laying his hand upon her shoulder.

She jerked his hand away.

"So marriage is the new idea with you, is it?" she asked, looking him in the eyes.

For a moment he lost his swagger. He recovered it quickly enough, however.

"Marriage has always been in my mind," he said. "It is only now, though, when I see a fortune arriving, that I feel the hour has come for my declaration."

"The fortune meaning," the girl exclaimed indignantly, "that you will take the roof from over my mother and father's heads and all my brothers' and

134

sisters', that you will take their land away, their farm! What is to become of them when I marry you, *Monsieur le Maire?*"

His tone became sullen.

"That is not my affair," he answered. "As for a 'dot,' I demand nothing. What has been saved for that purpose can help them to find another home. The only thing I will accept is the lease which is now cancelled of this house and lands bequeathed to me by my father. That, if it pleases you, Mother Dubler, I will take with me. As a matter of form it must be destroyed before the building commences."

Madame looked up. The young man began to feel uneasy. The atmosphere which his offer had created was not in the least what he had anticipated.

"So you want the lease back?"

"Why not?" he asked jauntily. "You have never paid one *sou*'s rent for the place. It has been nothing but waste-paper since the end of the first year. One does not occupy land for ever for which one pays nothing."

The door had been left partly open. There was the sound of voices outside, a knocking. General Besserley stood smiling at them all from the threshold. Behind him was the famous advocate.

"So this is the family, Madame," Besserley observed, looking around him with interest. "Mademoiselle Antoinette is an old friend. With Monsieur I have only exchanged a cursory greeting. And these are the children — yes? The young man — I am not mis-

135

taken — I believe I am addressing Monsieur Forniquot, the mayor of St. Marac?"

"That is so," the other answered. "Who are you?"

"I am a poor tramp," Besserley said, "who ate the best lunch he ever had in his life outside this house. I am better known, perhaps, as General Besserley of the Château de Villandry. This is my *avocat*, well known everywhere, I think, Maître Nessyen. We have brought back your lease, Madame."

"What do you mean — the lease?" Forniquot demanded. "It is worth nothing. The rent has never been paid. It has been valueless for years. It is nothing but a scrap of waste-paper. The property here is mine. I am the only son and I inherited everything my father left."

"Not quite so hasty, young man," Besserley begged. "You say that no rent has been paid. I dispute your statement. The rent has been fully paid up until next October."

"It is a lie!" he shouted. "Not one *sou* have I touched."

"It is the truth," Besserley replied. "My *avocat* here possesses the receipt for the money. It stands for the moment to the credit of your account at the Union Bank, Monte Carlo."

The lawyer drew the bank receipt from his pocket and read it out. Forniquot listened with bulging eyes. It was all madness, this, but a hundred thousand francs was something!

"Who are you?" he asked Besserley once more.

"Why have you paid this rent? How are you concerned in the matter at all?"

"A very reasonable question," Besserley replied. "I am concerned because I am a lover of the beauties of this part of the country. On a clear day this spot is visible from my Château. As it is the outlook is beautiful. If a hotel were built on this spot it would be hideous. When I discovered that there was a chance of something of the sort happening, I asked Madame to lend me the lease for my inspection. I found that it is a perfectly valid document and that the land is hers for another eighty-two years. It was necessary to put right the little trifle of the rent. That has been done."

"My client is stating the facts," Nessyen declared. "I shall presently hand over the receipt for these payments to you two good people. For the moment I had better, perhaps, preserve it. It is with the lease here in my possession. If I might offer my advice to the young man —— "

"To *Monsieur le Maire*," Forniquot interrupted angrily.

"To *Monsieur le Maire*," Nessyen corrected himself with an ironical little bow, "I would suggest that he go outside and break the news to those poor men who are wasting their time taking measurements and the architect who is also busy making an inspection. You will have to satisfy their claims for the time that has been wasted, no doubt, *Monsieur le Maire*, but that will not be a large affair."

Forniquot was still dazed.

"Do I understand you to say that the hundred thousand francs is paid to my credit at the Union Bank?" he demanded.

"The sum, which is even larger than that, was deposited a few hours ago," Nessyen replied. "You know who I am, without a doubt. You can accept my word for it."

The girl rose from her seat. She was a transformed being.

"Then I need not marry him!" she called out.

"God forbid that you should," her father answered. "We were too crushed to speak, but I should have wrung his neck first!"

"You are all going a little too fast," Forniquot said insolently. "I will go and talk to those men when I choose. After all, this house in which you find yourselves is my property."

"You lie," Dubler asserted. "My wife's grandfather built this house himself. Stone after stone he brought from the valley — he and one other man."

"It is built on my land."

"As regards that," Nessyen intervened, "there is a curious point which has come up, *Monsieur le Maire*, during the investigations of the last few days. There has been a great slackness in keeping books and registers connected with the common land, the rates, the taxes in all of the small towns of this *arrondissement*, and during your father's and your grandfather's time, Monsieur Forniquot, I fear that the authorities

138

of the place have been amongst the worst sinners in this respect. The State lawyers are at work investigating, but my own impression very clearly is that this land belongs to St. Marac. It is communal land for which the mayor of the place is trustee. I believe that your father was at fault in issuing that lease on his own account. It should have been issued on behalf of the *Commune* of the district."

"Then the hundred thousand francs —— " the young man gasped.

"I am afraid you will find that you will have to restore them to the *Commune*," Maître Nessyen declared. "That, however, is not an urgent matter. The investigations have only just commenced. I still think that this would be an opportune moment for you to explain to your friends outside that they are wasting their time."

Forniquot strode out of the house, but he carefully avoided the little crowd outside. He made his way to the path which led down to the lane where he had left his car. They called out to him. He only quickened his pace. Nessyen watched from the window. Dubler stood by his side. The children hurried through the open door. Antoinette, who had dried her eyes from those first tears of joy, took the two youngest each by hand and led them out. Madame had broken down. Besserley went over and patted her kindly on the shoulder.

"Come, come, Madame," he said, "you have had some rough times. They are over. You can believe Maître Nessyen, who is a great *avocat*. No one has any claim against this property now that the bank has given a receipt for the rent. The lease, too, being signed by Forniquot's father, either on his own behalf or on behalf of the *Commune*, is equally valid. No one will disturb you. Just think of that for a time and life will begin to look a little rosier. And you, Dubler," he went on, "you seem dazed, man! Come, I will give you something to do. Down in the road there is my automobile. Scramble down or send one of those lusty boys of yours and tell the chauffeur to bring up a hamper from there. We will sit outside on the bench and await you."

Father and boys hurried off down the path. Besserley passed his arm through the girl's and drew her out to the seat in front of the farmhouse.

"Tell me, Antoinette," he asked, "where is that tall, good-looking young rascal who was with you the first time we met?"

She laughed softly.

"I think he is somewhere down below waiting for *Monsieur le Maire!*" she said.

VII

MONSIEUR PIERRE ROUBILLON, editor and proprietor of the Nice *Daily Times*, which he frequently declared with belligerence and emphasis to be the finest journal published in Europe, seated in his conference room addressed with vigorous words his typist in chief and daughter, Marie Louise, his three sub-editors and two other members of the staff of little or no importance.

"This affair," he declared, banging the table in front of him with clenched fist, "will send me demented. The greatest item of news since 1914 is there ready to be scooped up and it eludes us. Some other journal will be more fortunate. We shall be disgraced. We shall lose our position. I ask myself what are my staff about?"

"Where is Cosperro?" one of the sub-editors asked.

"Fished out of Marseilles harbour with a boat hook, more dead than alive," Roubillon answered angrily. "He lies in the town hospital there. By the time he is discharged the whole affair will be ancient history."

"Young Boissevain then?"

"Shot through the shoulder for trespassing in the gardens of a villa near Paris. He will be brought up and charged with attempted burglary as soon as he leaves his room. Another bungler!"

"Our two best men," a sub-editor remarked dolefully.

"Then it is time we found better ones," Roubillon declared with a note of savagery in his tone. "Listen, all of you and let it be known amongst the news seekers of my staff: I give a reward of fifty thousand francs to anyone who can bring me the true story of what is happening on the yacht *Phallaris*, and what is to be the outcome of the deadlock in King Stephen's country. It is front-page news for every journal in Europe and not one word do we hear. Fifty thousand francs!"

"And if I get it," Marie Louise asked quietly, looking up from her machine, "may I have the fifty thousand francs and also marry Jacques?"

Monsieur Roubillon pushed his hand through his stiff upstanding white hair and glared at his daughter.

"You can have the fifty thousand francs and marry any idiot you choose if you bring me the news."

The sudden appearance of the *Phallaris*, the largest yacht which had ever entered Monaco Harbour, out of the morning mists created something of a sensation amongst the little crowd of loungers who always frequent the port. She had entered with a broad sweep from northwards and no one except the Harbour Master himself and the occupants of the villas high up on the northwards side had seen anything of her approach. For long after she had found her way to

142

the middle of the pool a continual stream of sightseers dribbled on to the broad promenade and docks to watch her take her place. The yacht owners who had their Lloyd's Registry handy turned over its pages fruitlessly. The boat was flying the American flag and the ensign of an unknown club. Her affiliations, if she had any, were unannounced. The crew of immaculately clad seamen, under the supervision of the captain and two or three other officers, brought her skilfully into position and then disappeared. Of the owner or his guests there was no evidence. There was an awning up, but no one underneath it. The usual crowd of nautically dressed young women in shorts or blue flannel trousers was absent. It was not until an hour after she had come to anchor that there were any signs of life on deck. Then the captain stepped into a launch, a stiff unresponsive figure, and was whirled across to the Harbour Master's office. A little later a smaller launch containing a young man who wore a yachting cap and a blue serge suit and was holding on to a carefully protected motor bicycle was landed at the nearest dock. He wasted no time answering enquiries from the small crowd who watched his arrival. He tested his machine, mounted it and rode off. The owner's portion of the luxuriously cushioned deck remained untenanted. There seemed to be nothing much else to wait for. The crowd of loiterers thinned; the girl dressed as a boy in blue fisherman's trousers and a jersey rose from the seat where she had been lying half curled up for the last two hours, made her way to the back of the café of the port and disappeared.

Up on the broad terrace of his mountain Château, General Besserley, who had just finished his swim, was taking vigorous exercise. In the midst of a complicated contortion of arms and legs, he suddenly stiffened and drew himself upright. The one sound for which he had the strongest dislike, the beating of a motor-cycle engine with an open exhaust, was distinctly audible. The rider of the machine was apparently mounting the hill and was already close at hand. Besserley slipped into his dressing-room, which opened out on to the terrace, and completed his toilet. Pierre, his valet, appeared just as he was about to ring for his morning coffee. He held out a note.

"A steward from a yacht which has just arrived in the harbour has brought this, sir," he announced. "They refused to let him pass at the lodge and told him that motor bicycles were not allowed on the estate."

"Quite right," Besserley growled. "Give me the note."

The valet obeyed. Besserley broke the seal and glanced it through, then he reread it and tore the sheet of paper into very small pieces which he consigned to the waste-paper basket.

"Send the young man up," he directed. "Tell him to leave his machine at the lodge. I will have my coffee outside in ten minutes."

Besserley, a fine, soldierly figure, notwithstanding his present-day life of country gentleman, stood on his terrace awaiting the visitor. The young man saluted as he climbed the last few steps.

"General Besserley?" he enquired.

Besserley nodded.

"When did you arrive?" he asked.

"About two hours ago, sir. My name is Broadhurst. I am one of the chief's secretaries."

"Well, you can tell the chief that I am entirely agreeable to his suggestion," Besserley said. "I have made all arrangements for his reception here, but I suppose upon the yacht more complete privacy is possible. At what time am I expected?"

"At about twelve o'clock, sir, if that will be convenient."

"Perfectly," Besserley agreed. "Will you take some coffee?"

The young man saluted.

"If you will excuse me, sir, I will be getting back," he replied. "Instructions were not to waste a moment after I had got into touch with you."

"How are your guests?"

"Quite all right, sir, considering the chief does not encourage their coming on deck until after dark."

"And the chief?"

The other hesitated.

"He is well, sir, but if I might say so he does seem exceptionally nervous."

"That's queer," Besserley remarked. "He's gone

145

through plenty of this sort of thing in his life."

"More than any man breathing, I should think," the visitor agreed. "He is very anxious to get into conference with you as quickly as possible."

"I shall be down punctually at midday. Everything going all right?"

"Very well indeed, I should say, General. It is the Press who have been giving us the most trouble. We had a dreadful time with them in Marseilles and we had a boat load following us all the way to Toulon. The wireless, too, is going continuously but, of course, we take no notice of that."

"Do you think that they have come to any decision?" Besserley asked.

"Hard to say, sir," the youth replied. "We see scarcely anything of them. I will tell the chief, then, sir, to expect you at midday."

"I shall be there," Besserley promised.

The messenger hesitated in the act of turning away.

"By the by, sir," he said, "someone passed me like a whirlwind coming up the hill on a perfectly lovely little machine. I saw it just inside the wood as I stopped at the lodge gates."

"Machine? What are you talking about?"

"Motor bike, sir. Mine's pretty good but not a patch on this one."

"What — here — in the wood here?"

"Just close to your last lodge, sir. The one with the huge iron gates where they stopped me."

Besserley rang the bell.

146

"This young gentleman tells me that there is a motor bicycle in a corner of the wood opposite the entrance to the lodge," he said to the butler. "Have you heard anything about it?"

"Yes, sir," was the respectful reply. "I have just had a telephone message. No one knows to whom it belongs. Whoever left it there must be in the wood."

"Have the place searched," Besserley ordered. "Anyone you find trespassing bring up here."

"Very good, sir."

The young man took his leave. Besserley sat down to his *petit déjeuner* in a somewhat unhappy frame of mind. There was nothing as a rule that gave him more genuine satisfaction than to be engaged in any enterprise of an unusual nature, especially when it was to further a cause of which he approved or to benefit any of his friends. The present enterprise, however, had never greatly appealed to him. Even at this late hour nothing would have given him more pleasure than to have wiped his hands of the whole affair. His connection with it involved him in no danger, financial or personal, the adventure to which he was committed made no drastic call even upon his intelligence and yet, as he sat smoking his after-breakfast pipe, he decided that he was weary of the *Phallaris*, he was bored with his distinguished countryman — association with whom even to a man of Besserley's position was without doubt a great honour — and he had lost his enthusiasm for the whole business — including the two principals. He had, in fact, just come to the conclusion that any interruption whatever would be a relief, when he looked up to find one which was certainly not calculated to soothe his ruffled nerves. Two of the *gardes-chasse* were approaching and between them walked, with a somewhat swaggering gait, a young person who showed signs of having been engaged in a fracas of some sort with her escort.

"We found this person in the woods, sir," one of the *gardes* announced indignantly. "She was right up amongst my young pheasants."

Besserley stared at the captive for a moment and then frowned. Next to his aversion to motor bicycles came an unswerving dislike of seeing women in trousers.

"Are you a girl?" he asked.

"Can you not see that?" she replied. "Of course I am."

He looked at her for a moment with utter distaste. Her dark-brown hair was disarranged and she was still breathing hard from the exertion of running.

"You do not seem to like me," she remarked blandly. "Is it my clothes?"

"I dislike your attire very much," he confessed, "but that is rather beside the question."

"I do not think they are becoming myself," she admitted with a disapproving look at her trousers. "I am too thin, of course, but I have rather a nice figure and these things are badly cut."

"What makes you wear them, then?" he asked.

"Well, I had to wear something."

Besserley changed the subject precipitately.

"Perhaps you wouldn't mind telling me what you were doing in my woods?" he enquired.

"Trying to find a place to hide."

"Why?"

"Oh, I felt sure that something was going to happen up here and I wanted to find out what it was."

"So that's it," he said quietly. "Don't you think, if you wanted to escape observation, you were rather foolish to leave that wretched machine of yours leaning against the hedge?"

"Of course I do," she agreed. "I did not know there would be so many people poking about — and it is not a wretched machine. It's the most beautiful one that has ever been made. They told me so at the factory."

"Young ladies do not ride such things," he told her severely.

She sighed.

"Another dream shattered! I can never be a young lady."

Besserley abandoned the discussion. His unwilling visitor looked around her approvingly. The appointments of his breakfast-table, the choice china, the old silver and the bowl of roses in the centre, were all appealing.

"How good your coffee smells," she continued, with a little sniff.

"Perhaps you have been out all night?" he suggested.

149

"No, I have not been here long," she assured him. "I followed the man who came from the yacht."

"Why?"

She shrugged her shoulders.

"You are getting inquisitive. If you really insist upon knowing, I wanted to find out at what time your guests were arriving."

"I will set your curiosity at rest," he confided. "My guests are not arriving at all. How you knew I was going to have any I cannot imagine. That is of no consequence. The plans are changed."

"So I have had my ride for nothing," she complained.

He called to Henri who was lingering in the background.

"Another cup and some more rolls," he ordered. "You fellows can go now," he added, turning to the *gardes*. "The plans for the day are altered. You need not remain on special duty, and the gates can be unlocked at the back of the estate. My visitors will not arrive."

The men saluted and withdrew. Henri departed on his errand.

"Now you are beginning to talk like a human being," the girl remarked as she seated herself.

"I don't think you'll like the way I am going to talk in a minute or two," he told her.

"Put it off as long as you can," she begged. "Do not let anything spoil the first sip of my coffee. Is it really General Besserley whose hospitality I am accepting?"

"It is."

"You are the world-famed American soldier and diplomat who lives alone in this marvellous Château and gives amazing parties and knows kings and prime ministers?"

"A little exuberant," he observed, "but I am the man."

"Dear me," she murmured, "and to think that I am taking my *petit déjeuner* with you!"

She accepted her cup and waited while Henri poured out the coffee. Then she added some sugar and milk and Besserley noticed that her fingers were very delicate and well kept.

"Here are rolls and butter and toast, honey and some preserves. Will you help yourself? As soon as you have finished I shall be sending you down to the *Gendarmerie*."

"*Mais non!*" she protested, buttering her roll. "You would not be so cruel. I may seem greedy, but I cannot help it. I had just ordered my breakfast when that young man left the yacht with his bicycle and I had to follow him."

"That brings us back to the question — why?"

"I am a spy," she confided.

"They don't exist nowadays," he said scornfully. "I believe you are really one of the most contemptible things in the world."

"What is that?"

"A young-lady journalist who does not know her job."

She went on with her breakfast for a moment or two without speaking. Her appetite seemed to have diminished.

"*Touché*," she admitted presently. "You may be the great General Besserley but I do not like the way you talk to a poor girl who is starving and has to accept your hospitality."

"You are lucky not to be accepting the hospitality of the police," he told her.

"There really is not any need to be so disagreeable," she argued. "Why cannot you tell me all about what is happening on the yacht and then I will go away quite peaceably?"

"You will go peaceably, anyhow, as soon as you have finished your breakfast."

"Then I shall make it last a very long time."

Besserley lit a cigarette and leaned back in his chair.

"As soon as I consider that a reasonable time has elapsed," he confided, "I shall call back the *gardes-chasse*."

She helped herself to a second roll.

"I would not," she advised. "They are quite happy where they are."

"The levity of your tone and manner," he observed, "borders upon the disrespectful."

She laughed softly.

"Why have I to be respectful?" she enquired.

"You are not a magistrate, you are not even a French soldier. I was found in your woods. That means a small fine, at the worst."

"So you think you will get off with that, do you?"

"I think so," she replied. "You know you are putting all this on, General Besserley, or else you are in a particularly bad humour to-day. Everyone says you are one of the kindest men alive. You would not bring disgrace upon a young girl by sending her to prison."

Besserley rose to his feet and walked the length of the terrace several times. When he returned he rang for Henri and summoned one of the *gardes*.

"Look here," he ordered the latter. "You march this lady to that bicycle of hers, see her on it and start her off for wherever she wants to go. If you find her on the estate again don't come and worry me about it. Take her straight to the *Gendarmerie*. You understand?"

"*Entendu, Monsieur*," the man replied.

The girl rose to her feet.

"I knew you were not really so bad," she declared. "You would not like to give me a cigarette to smoke going home?"

"Certainly not. I hate to see girls of your age smoking."

"I am not quite so young as I look," she ventured.

He took no notice. She came a little nearer to him.

"You would not care to shake hands, I suppose, and let me say thank you?"

He drew himself up. He was really a very tall man

153

and notwithstanding a certain elegance of figure she was a very small girl.

"I do not wish to shake hands with you," he said, "or ever to see you again."

"You will not tell me anything about who is on the yacht?"

"Off you go!" he ordered sternly. "The last chance, mind!"

She sighed and turned away. A few minutes later he heard the hideous sound of her engine with its open exhaust as she raced down the private road.

"Help, please! Help! Quickly — I drown!"

A very beautiful lady who had been lounging on a luxurious divan in the salon of her suite on the *Phallaris* jumped to her feet, cautiously pulled back the curtain from the porthole and peeped out. Just below her a girl in fisherman's clothes, who seemed on the point of exhaustion, was treading water feebly. She caught sight of the face and called out again with renewed vigour.

"*Madame, je vous prie!* They will not take me on board, but I choke. I am drowning! Please tell them to throw me a rope or something."

"Hold on for a moment," the lady cried. "I will fetch help. It shall arrive immediately."

She rang every bell she could see, flung open the door of her suite and ran up the companionway. An officer on guard apparently at the outside door looked at her in something like horror.

"Madame!" he expostulated.

"Can you not hear her? There is a girl drowning by the side of the yacht!"

"I saw her," the man admitted. "I whistled for a boat. It will be here directly."

"You are inhuman," was the indignant response. "Let down the gangway. There it is — only a yard away."

The officer hesitated.

"Madame, if the boat is not in time I will jump overboard. But consider, I do not believe that the girl drowns. To bring her on board is to break our sworn word. The boat will land her anywhere she chooses. It will be here this moment."

"*C'est scandaleux!*" the lady shrieked. "The gangway! I insist. Listen — I insist. Obey my orders!"

The officer turned unwillingly away. With his own hands he swung round the gangway, undid the fastening until it touched the water. With three strokes of amazing power for such an exhausted young woman, the girl in the water reached it. She climbed up but found her progress barred at the top.

"There is a boat coming round," the officer told her. "If you will hold on to my arm —— "

She pushed him away, she swayed on her feet and looked pleadingly at the lady barely visible standing a few steps down the companionway.

"Madame," she implored, "I faint! I have no breath."

Madame's orders were not to be misunderstood.

The officer stood away. The girl stumbled across the few yards of deck with outstretched hands. The lady supported her down the companionway.

"I ruin your clothes," the girl faltered. "Madame — bless you!"

"What do my clothes matter?" was the compassionate reply. "You poor child — and how brutal that man was. Gently — there, lie down on the divan."

The girl shrank away.

"But, Madame," she protested, "look! I make a pool of water. I spoil your beautiful carpet."

"I am accustomed to be obeyed. Lie down."

Madame threw a rug over the girl and turned to one of the stewards who seemed to be streaming into the room.

"Brandy," she ordered. "Go away, the rest of you. Annette will do what I want. Brandy and something hot — and fetch the doctor."

"You will not turn me away until you have spoken to me again?" the girl pleaded.

"That I swear I will not do," was the prompt reply. "Officer!"

The man, standing in a state of helpless uncertainty at the top of the companionway, took a step downwards.

"You will accept an order from me?"

"Naturally, Madame," he replied. "Have I not already done so?"

"The young woman is to remain exactly where she is while I go and change my frock. You understand?

My maid will be with her to see that she has everything necessary and that the doctor looks after her. On no account is she to leave the ship until I return."

"Madame will protect my disobedience?"

She smiled.

"Have no fear," she said. "Circumstances have changed."

Marie Louise also smiled faintly and closed her eyes. She was really rather exhausted, not so much from her struggles with the sea as because she was really a somewhat indifferent actress.

At twelve o'clock that morning, Besserley, in his own little launch from the other side of the harbour, boarded the yacht. He was received by the captain and ushered into the saloon, where he was welcomed by his old friend, ex-Ambassador Richard Grantley, multi-millionaire of worldwide reputation, owner of the *Phallaris* and one of the most accomplished diplomats breathing.

"Forgive us for upsetting your plans, Besserley," he said as he shook hands. "The fact of it is, we are all in a state of nerves here — or rather have been. You must let me present you to His Majesty King Stephen."

Stephen, a good-looking young man with a humorous smile, excellent features and sunburnt complexion, greeted the newcomer warmly.

"I have heard of you often, General," he acknowledged. "I can scarcely conceive any other country than America who could afford to keep two such men as you and Grantley behind the scenes. Now that I have spent the best part of three days with Grantley and studied your correspondence with him on my affairs, however, I begin to understand that it may be possible to achieve great things in an unusual manner."

"Your Majesty flatters us," Besserley replied. "Richard Grantley, of course, continues to be the unofficial ambassador of the United States wherever he sets his foot. I can claim nothing of that sort of distinction myself, but there are times, I think, when one can accomplish more if one has not an official position."

"I do not think," Stephen said thoughtfully, "that anyone could have reconciled apparently irreconcilable issues with the same skill as you, my two friends, have shown in dealing with my affairs. There are two important points left, however, for which we have awaited your coming."

Grantley led the way into his private cabin. The three men seated themselves at a small round table.

"I will now explain," Grantley began, "just why I have kept this meeting secret from everyone and have adopted very severe measures with regard to one or two over-zealous journalists who have endeavoured to intrude. The fact is that certain negotiations in connection with His Majesty which we three are bringing, I hope, to a successful termination, would have been, as you, Besserley, were the first to point out, stoutly opposed by the relatives and advisers of the Queen if the slightest whisper concerning the nature of our efforts had been permitted to drift into the Press."

Stephen nodded with shrewd understanding.

"That, so far, has been a continual stumbling block in our way," he admitted.

"Nevertheless," Grantley continued, "here, and without any outside influences brought to bear, I think that we — I, viva voce, and Besserley in those very convincing letters of his — have presented the matter to your spouse, sire, in such a way that she takes for the first time an altered view of the situation. She knows everything that has to be known, she has taken twenty-four hours to consider the whole affair from a different angle and she has promised to let us have her answer the moment you, Besserley, arrived. In any case I am now content. Her Majesty has had the situation presented to her in clearly written and clearly expressed phraseology from my friend Besserley. She has also spent many hours discussing with me various points upon which her attitude has been a little biased. All I can say to you, sire, and to you, Besserley, is that I am hoping for the best."

"You are a wonderful fellow, Grantley," Stephen declared. "I shall just put a word in here, if I may. If Catherine is really content to view the situation as I have always viewed it, if you two have brought her round even a little to our way of thinking, Grantley, trifles shall never interfere with the wonderful result. I, too, shall be content and happy to meet my wife half-way."

"I pass on now," the ex-Ambassador proceeded, "to our own side of the question. A great deal of money is necessary to put the finances of your country, sire, in order. A great deal of money shall be placed at your disposal. I have accepted another suggestion of our friend Besserley's which I may say His Majesty has welcomed. The government of his country as vested in King Stephen is to have an interest and a share of control in every one of the concessions which he is signing, I hope to-day, in our favour. There they are — eleven concessions — and one more formal document to be signed by yourself, sire, and Her Majesty, which is an assurance of your complete and permanent reconciliation. A copy of the latter is already in Her Majesty's possession."

Stephen rose to his feet.

"You have done everything that is possible, gentlemen," he admitted. "It is now, I presume, as you say in your country, up to me."

"If you will have the few necessary words with Her Majesty, sire," Grantley said, "you will find General Besserley and myself in the saloon at your disposal."

The round table in the saloon where luncheon and dinner were usually served was laid for four people, and beautifully decorated with flowers and glass. Several gold-foiled bottles in ice-pails were in evidence.

Grantley led his companion to a smaller table adjoining, where a secretary had been laying out a row of documents and writing materials.

"I wonder," Besserley remarked thoughtfully, with a glance across at the festive arrangements, "how long these young people will be."

"Just the length of time that we shall require, I think," Grantley replied, with a nod to the chief steward who was standing in the background.

The music of shaken ice was promptly audible. The ship's cocktail was duly drunk. It was no sooner finished than there was a little commotion at the entrance. Stephen and his wife entered hand in hand. It seemed to the two men that Catherine had never appeared more beautiful. Stephen, too, had the air of a bridegroom.

"I take it, sire, that the nature of your entrance is meant as an allegory?" Grantley asked with a respectful salutation and a glance at the linked fingers.

"I am delighted to tell you that Her Majesty and I are in entire accord," was the gracious reply.

They sank into chairs. Besserley, who was an old friend, paid his respects to the Queen. Grantley remained standing before the smaller table.

"The first document which you are signing, Sire and Madame," he said, "is your formal agreement to reconciliation upon the terms which you have both read and approved. Will you allow me?"

He handed a gold pen to Madame, another to the King. They both glanced down the sheet and signed.

161

"You have each had a copy of this," Grantley went on. "The original will remain for the present in my keeping. There is nothing left but for His Majesty to sign the various concessions for the silver and quicksilver mines and the oil production wherever it shall be decided to sink wells. General Besserley and I will then sign on behalf of our country the agreement to carry out our part of the bargain and to transfer the first sum payable on account of the concessions to the credit of your National Bank."

The business of signatures was swiftly concluded. Afterwards they moved to the larger table and took their places. Grantley remained standing with his glass in his hand.

"My friends," he said quietly, "if I may presume to address you as such, our period of probation is ended. At midnight a rocket will be fired from this boat which nobody will understand but ourselves. It will mean that all secrecy is at an end. We shall issue a statement to the Press within twenty-four hours, and it will be my great privilege to take my passengers no longer in a prison, but on, I trust, a real pleasure cruise to the shores of their country. You will permit me," he concluded, "to wish long life and a happy continuance of their reign to King Stephen and Queen Catherine!"

Stephen leaned over and took his wife's hand once more. At that moment there was a sound of a slight report and a flare from the Minstrels' Gallery. They looked up at it in surprise. A slim, girlish figure was leaning over the rail, a figure which disappeared immediately afterwards with incredible haste.

"Who is that?" Grantley demanded.

"It is the young woman we rescued from the sea," Catherine declared. "She asked to be allowed to have her clothes dried and she seems to have borrowed my camera. She appeared to know all about our little affair and she was so charmingly interested that so long as it was all settled I lent her my copy of the agreement."

"It's that damned girl again!" Besserley exclaimed, forgetful for a moment of his whereabouts.

But for the ripple of laughter and explanations which followed they might have heard, soon after, the throb of a motor engine with the exhaust fully open as Marie Louise sped along the quay on her way to Nice with a copy of the vital document in her pocket and the golden vision of fifty thousand francs and a marriage licence always before her enraptured eyes.

VIII

A GENDARME stepped out into the road and stopped General Besserley's limousine on the Middle Corniche a few kilometres out of Nice. Its owner leaned out of the window.

"Anything wrong?" he enquired.

The gendarme recognized his questioner and saluted.

"I would take the lower road home to-night, if I were you, sir," he advised. "A man has already been robbed between here and Eze."

"Robbed?" Besserley repeated. "That is an unusual event, is it not?"

"It happens from time to time, sir," was the reluctant reply. "The *Commissaire* has been notified and we are expecting the sergeant presently."

"Well, I think I'll take my chance," Besserley decided.

"As you will, sir. We have received instructions to warn motorists. It is quite possible, of course, that as one robbery has taken place nothing more will happen."

Besserley signalled the chauffeur to drive on. They were within a couple of kilometres of Eze when the brakes were suddenly applied. The car came to a standstill and a dark figure was visible through the open window.

"*Haut les mains!*"

Besserley raised one arm a little too quickly for the youth who had planted himself outside. He received the full weight of Besserley's knuckles at exactly the right place — under the chin. A very old-fashioned revolver which he had been brandishing clattered into the road and the aggressor himself collapsed with scarcely a groan. The chauffeur descended and opened the door. He was a man of few words, which is perhaps why he had held his post for some fifteen years.

"Shall I put him in front and run him up to La Turbie *Gendarmerie*, sir?" he enquired.

Besserley stepped out on to the road.

"Let's have a look at him," he proposed.

He bent over the fallen man and felt for a moment a slight sense of shame. In broad daylight a slap on the cheek would have been the best answer to this young man's impertinent demand. He was thin to the point of emaciation, as pale as death and his attire was that of a bar lounger rather than a brigand.

"Mistaken his vocation," Besserley murmured.

"I will put him up with me in the front, anyway, sir."

Besserley shook his head.

"I'll have him inside," he decided. "Put him there in the corner opposite me. That's right. He's coming-to fast. Wait a minute."

Besserley drew a flask from a side pocket, unscrewed it, poured a little of its contents into the silver cup and forced it between the unconscious man's lips. In a moment or two he showed signs of recovery. He opened his eyes and groaned.

"Feeling better?"

No reply. There was the dawn of an expression in the eyes, however, and that expression was fear.

"Drive along until we come to the mountain road," Besserley told the chauffeur. "You can pull up there. Dare say I shall have made up my mind what to do with him by that time."

"Shall I look him over and see if he has got a weapon, sir?"

Besserley smiled.

"To judge by the one he was brandishing, he would not know how to use it if he had. I'll keep my eye on him."

They started on again slowly. Besserley took further note of his captive. He was a young man apparently of about twenty-five years, shabbily dressed and of unpleasant appearance.

"Well, I see you are recovering," his vis-à-vis remarked. "Here I am with my hands up. What do you want?"

The youth scowled. His courage, however, had departed with his first challenge. He was a cheap creature of shams.

"I want food, wine, cigarettes and money."

"Well, that's easy. You don't expect me to have all the luxuries of life with me in the car, though, do you?"

"You have the money," the other replied. "Hand that over and I will see about the rest."

Besserley chuckled. Perhaps his victim was not so bad after all. There had been a touch of humour about the way he had delivered himself of his little speech.

"Are you the fierce robber I was told was loose upon the road?"

"I took a pocket-book from a commercial traveller," was the dreary reply. "It contained four francs fifty. He had nothing else fit to touch. He started running while I was counting the cash and I should think he has reached Nice by now."

"Not a good day for a professional," Besserley observed.

"First time I ever stole anything," was the sullen retort.

"What is your occupation?"

"Gigolo."

"Not for the moment enjoying the best of good fortune, I presume?"

"Rub it in! I'm starving — so is my girl."

"Where is she?"

"That's no business of yours."

"H'm. You are scarcely an amiable companion," Besserley commented.

"I didn't force myself upon you. I'm dead out of luck. That's what's wrong. You're the sort of fellow I would stumble up against just because I had summoned up a little courage and made up my mind to go through with the thing."

167

"Yes, you were out of luck there," the other agreed. "I don't allow people to rob me. On the other hand —— "

"What other hand?"

"On the other hand," Besserley continued smoothly, "I am known far and wide as an easy mark for suppliants — what is generally called a philanthropist."

"Then fork out a *mille*," the young man suggested. "I would rather have a little money than this palaver."

"Very natural. Still, I must understand a little more about you before I part. Supposing I produced the *mille*, what would you do? Buy a new suit of clothes and present yourself at the Nice casino?"

The ex-gigolo shivered.

"No more Nice for me," he muttered.

"Well, Monte Carlo, then?"

"I should like to start in Monte Carlo. That's where Lula wanted to start, anyhow."

"Who is Lula?"

"My girl. At least, she is not my girl but I call her that, anyway."

"Well, where is she? If you have a girl who is as down and out as you are, we ought to do something about it."

They had reached the turn. Besserley touched his communicating phone.

"Go on up to the Château, Paul," he ordered.

There was silence for a few minutes. Then the ex-gigolo spoke again.

"What are you going to do with me when we get to your blasted Château?"

"From the force of your language," Besserley remarked, "I should judge you to be an American."

"Well, you're one yourself."

"Precisely, but happily of a different type. I can use language, too, if I try," Besserley added, and there was rather a steely glint in his eyes. "You know that I can use my fists quickly. I am pretty nimble on my feet, too, and although I am quite sure that I am frequently called 'easy,' I can be — the reverse."

"Oh, you can be the tough guy all right, I'm sure of that," the ex-gigolo muttered. "What I want to know is what you are going to do with me at your — Château?"

"I am going to hand you over to my servant," Besserley replied. "You will have a bath, be provided with clothes, including fresh linen and underwear; afterwards you will be fed, given some wine and some cigarettes. At the end of that time I shall interview you again."

"Christ!"

"And," Besserley concluded, "although I have been used to hearing a good deal of powerful language in my life, I do not really like it. You will probably think it worth your while to bear that in mind."

The young man turned uneasily in his place. A bend in the road had brought them within view of the Château, a fine spectacle with its long row of blazing lights and its dimly seen outline.

"Is that where you are taking me?" he asked.

"Yes."

"Crikey!"

Besserley nodded in mild approval.

"As an anathema," he said, "crikey is anæmic but expressive. Follow me into the hall."

The other did as he was bidden. It was noticeable that neither Henri nor his subordinate, who were both awaiting the arrival of the car, showed the slightest surprise at the entrance of this unusual visitor.

"Send for Pierre," Besserley directed.

The valet was there almost like magic. Besserley explained what was to be done with the newcomer.

"But first of all," he added, "give him one glass of sherry and two biscuits, and he can smoke a cigarette while you are changing him if he wants to."

The master of the Château made his way to his study. He saw no more of the ex-gigolo for an hour and a half. At the end of that time, just as he was thinking of having his own bath and changing for dinner, Pierre returned with his charge. Besserley looked the latter over critically and smiled.

"Feeling better?" he asked.

"Who wouldn't be?" the young man replied. "I've had two glasses of sherry and a plateful of biscuits."

"Spoil your dinner."

His guest, who was looking vastly improved in a neat grey suit, clean linen and a restrained tie, his hair brushed, his chin smoothly shaven, grinned.

"Am I going to have some dinner?"

"In about three-quarters of an hour. What about Lula?"

"She's at Beaulieu."

"What is she doing there?"

"Waiting. I know a woman who has a room to let there. She took the bus from Nice. I went up on the Corniche to try my luck. I didn't tell her what I was thinking of."

"Well, what do you want to do about Lula?" Besserley asked.

"I should like her to have some dinner somewhere," was the candid reply.

Besserley considered the matter.

"Look here," he said, "I will send for Lula if you like. You write a note and tell her to come with the chauffeur, then I will hear this hard-luck story of yours. At the worst I will give you dinner, rooms for the night and a trifle to start you on with in the morning and pack you off. If you've got a story that appeals to me in any way I will see whether it is possible to help you."

"What could be fairer?" the young man murmured, reverting to the slang of a past generation.

"Sit down and write the note and address it," Besserley told him, pointing to a desk. "Pierre, order out a small car. It is only for Beaulieu and back."

"Very good, sir."

The ex-gigolo wrote the note and handed it to Pierre with full instructions for the chauffeur.

"I shall now leave you alone," Besserley said, "for half an hour or so. By the by, what is your name?"

The other winced.

"Gilbert," he confided.

"And the young lady's — apart from Lula?"

"She is an Egyptian by birth. I know very little about her. I met her on the boat last week crossing from Alexandria to Marseilles. Her name is Lula Fehrend."

"You are not married, then, or anything of that sort?"

The ex-gigolo whose name was Gilbert shook his head.

"Lula isn't the marrying sort," he said calmly. "Besides, she wouldn't touch me with a pair of tongs."

"The morning papers are there," Besserley pointed out. "I shall be down in three quarters of an hour."

"Thank you, sir."

Besserley made his way upstairs to where Pierre had prepared his bath. He suffered himself to be divested of his clothing and disappeared in a cloud of steam. He sat in the bath for an unusually long time and every now and then he grinned.

"Once more," he said to himself, "I can clearly see that I am about to make a damn' fool of myself!"

The young lady had arrived when Besserley descended once more to the study. His first impressions of her were entirely negative. She was very pale, a pallor that was more noticeable as she seemed to make use of no cosmetics whatever. Her eyes were the deepest and the largest he had ever seen in any girl's face. Her figure was much slimmer than the typical Egyptian's and her little bow as he entered the room had a grace of its own. She spoke in rather hesitating English and there was something curious about her voice which for some time he was unable to analyze.

"You are being very kind to me, General Besserley," she said.

"Well, I have not done much about it yet," he replied smiling. "Sent a car to fetch you up to dinner."

"A very beautiful car," she continued, "and yours is a very beautiful Château, and I do not know why you should give us dinner. Gilbert has confessed everything to me. He has told me he tried to rob you. I told him he was very foolish not to start with someone smaller."

Her little laugh was like music. Besserley listened to it with pleasure.

"Perhaps I ought to confess," he said. "I had been warned. A gendarme had told me a short time before that there was a dangerous robber on the road with an armoury of revolvers who had just succeeded in robbing one man of — I forget how much it was — and he was hanging about for me. Naturally I was prepared."

"You did not use weapons at all," she laughed. "Gilbert told me that you knocked him down and it was very painful. His chin is still sore."

"Oh, well, he'll soon get over that," Besserley replied.

Henri's understudy had entered with a trayful of cocktails. The girl shook her head. Gilbert and his host helped themselves.

"No cocktail?" the latter asked.

"I have never tasted one," she said. "I have never tasted wine. I have not any desire. I have seen so many people who seem to talk differently after they have drunk cocktails and if they talk differently they must think differently. I shall wait."

Besserley looked at his glass reflectively for a moment, then threw back his head and swallowed its contents.

"Well," he remarked, "at your age I think you are very wise."

"Lula is very strict and simple in her tastes," Gilbert confided. "She knows quite well that she has very unusual gifts. She is afraid of interfering with them. I understand her so little that I do not argue. In all things I believe that she knows best."

Again the girl smiled.

"That is not like an American man, is it, General Besserley?" she asked. "Not like an Englishman, either. I have not met many men but they all seem to think that they know much more than we do. Perhaps they are right."

"You know you don't think so," Gilbert declared.

"No," she admitted, "I do not think so. It is not the fault of the man. He has very little time in life for contemplation. He has to work and sometimes his work develops his brain the wrong way. Contemplation is always good spiritually."

Dinner was served in a room opening from the study. The girl gave a little exclamation of delight as she saw the table with its beautiful glass and flowers and exquisitely wrought Italian linen.

"But it is beautiful!" she cried softly. "I have never seen anything so beautiful. We are to sit at table there?"

Besserley pointed to her chair on his right which a servant was holding. She drew a long breath of content.

"This," she said, "is the way to live — amongst beautiful, really beautiful things. I am very happy."

Besserley, a self-confessed epicurean, had made a fine art of the niceties of living. His cuisine, his wines and his service were as near perfection as possible, and he took care that the environment itself was in harmony. He watched his two guests curiously. The young man was frankly greedy, but he exercised a certain restraint when it came to drinking the wines, so that although he gained in confidence, the whole of the time he kept his head. The girl ate with delicacy but showed a fine appreciation of the choice foods and of the elegance of her surroundings. She talked very little; she seemed most of the time absorbed in a sort of Nirvana of thought, acutely conscious of everything that was passing and of everything she saw and tasted, and yet with a deliberate abstention from speech except where it was necessary. The meal was half-way through when she suddenly leaned towards her host.

"I have never drunk wine in my life," she confided. "Some day I know that I must. I would like to begin. I would like some of that fine golden wine in this beautiful glass," she said, fingering a tall Hock glass faintly amber-tinted and with scrollwork of a deeper gold. "May I?"

"For one who knows nothing of wines, young lady, you have made an excellent choice," Besserley approved. "That is a Berncastler Doctor, a German wine, unfortunately rather scarce in these days."

Henri had already filled her glass. Besserley answered her gesture and raised his own.

"I can think of no toast worthy of such an occassion," he regretted, smiling.

"I can think of only one wish," she replied. "That I may never be asked to drink again until I can drink something as delightful. . . ."

They moved back into the study for their coffee. Lula established herself in a corner of the divan close to Besserley's easy chair. The young man sat opposite. Conversation at first was a little hampered by the passing of servants with liqueurs and coffee-cups. As soon as they were alone together Besserley turned in his chair and looked at his neighbour.

"Tell me, my guest with dreaming eyes," he enjoined, "what you are thinking of when you look into another face so intently?"

She laughed very quietly.

"You are asking me now," she said, "the secret of my life."

Her eyes met his without quivering. For a moment they seemed to lose expression, to become glacial, though their beauty remained. Then they became soft again. There was something of enquiry in their depths, something indefinable in the disturbance which they caused. Suddenly the boy's voice rang out on a sharp, angry note.

"Lula!" he exclaimed. "It is forbidden!"

There was silence in the room. The girl was sitting quite still, exactly like an image. Besserley was frankly astonished. The young man was pale and angry.

"Hello, what's the matter?" his host demanded, vaguely conscious in himself that there was something wrong.

"She knows," Gilbert answered, moving his head in her direction. "It is forbidden, Lula."

Her little laugh rippled like music into the room.

"What a foolish young man you are!" she exclaimed. "As though your little words, your small thoughts, your forbidding, could make any difference! Stupid — very stupid, Gilbert. But I will please you because you have brought me here."

"And to-morrow," he said, "I had meant to take you away without a word. I have changed my mind. General Besserley, you would like to know our story — or rather hers? It will take me exactly two minutes, and when I have finished you will not believe me."

"This sounds intriguing," Besserley confessed, lighting the largest cigar he had been able to find and taking a sip of his brandy. "Yes, I should like to hear the story. What is it? Two minutes of drama, tragedy, comedy — what?"

"I believe," the girl said, "that it will be two minutes of the truth, and what the truth is he does not know, and you do not know, and I do not think that I know."

"The fact of it is, sir," Gilbert began, "that young woman sitting by your side is only half human. You may believe me or not. I know what I am talking about. They used to say in Cairo that she came from a race of priestesses. I don't know what they were — mummies, funny people — but they used also to say, and that I know to be true, that she has inherited something that no living man or woman can properly explain. You would have to go back to the tombs, back to behind Tutankhamen to find out all about her."

Besserley knocked off the first ash from his cigar a little prematurely — an unusual thing with him. He had turned his shoulder away from the girl.

"Go on," he invited cheerfully.

"Lula and I and an old Egyptian woman, her servant, who died a few nights after we left Alexandria, arrived in Nice only last week," he went on. "I was a dancer; Lula sometimes danced with me, but she had a little money and I had none and sometimes she refused to dance. We went into the casino at Nice. It was there I found out. She sat by my side one night and she watched the game. I lost my money — of course I lost it. She whispered to me: 'You are foolish. What number are you backing next?'

" 'Seven,' I told her.

" 'Seven,' she repeated. 'Seven.'

178

"She did nothing. She did not move — that I can swear — but she looked steadily at the croupier, and presently I saw him turn as though unwillingly to her, and he looked at her, and for second after second he never moved his eyes. Then he bent forward over the wheel and just as he was going to spin it he looked away again. Lula was looking at him, and again he was staring at her and his fingers — I saw all this and I am not an imaginative person — his fingers were shaking. Then he turned, he muttered the usual croak and the ball spun, and when he called the number it was almost under his voice. It was seven. I had won thirty-five louis."

There was a dead silence.

"This sounds interesting," Besserley observed.

"There is very little more of it," Gilbert replied. "I went on playing but Lula did not speak to me. I had moderate luck, but by degrees my pile was dwindling away. Lula was not playing herself. She was staring at the board. At last she spoke to me.

" 'What number are you backing this time?'

"I had recovered from that queer little shock when seven had turned up and I just smiled. I doubled seven in my head."

" 'Fourteen,' I told her. 'I am going to plunge, Lula.' "

"And what happened?" Besserley asked.

"Exactly the same pantomime. I put a hundred francs on the number, I put twenty on all the *chevaux* and twenty on all the *carrés*. I saw the croupier staring again at Lula as though unwillingly. I saw that queer little smile Lula has sometimes on her lips and her eyes seemed to grow, they were so large. Only once she looked away and that was at the board, at the number and then back to the croupier and he was there waiting. When her eyes had met his again he spun. Fourteen turned up. He got through his announcement and then I thought he was going to fall over the wheel. He sat up and touched the chef, whispered in his ear. The chef nodded and called one of the relief men. The croupier left the table."

Besserley took another sip of brandy. He smoked quite fast for several seconds.

"Look here, young fellow," he said, "are you trying to make me believe that this girl could impose her will upon that board through the croupier?"

"I am only telling you," was the savage reply, "what happened. We were asked to leave the casino. There was no reason given. They were very polite but they just didn't want us. We went across to the Jetée Casino. For some time Lula would do nothing. She did not speak to me. Then she leaned towards me and pointed to a number — sixteen. I backed it, and again that little pantomime went on. The croupier became suddenly uneasy. He looked at Lula and seemed unable to look away. He hesitated a long time before he would spin. When he did, sixteen turned up."

"And how long did this go on?" Besserley asked.

"It didn't go on at all," Gilbert replied. "A messenger came over from the town casino — I recognized

him at once. One of the chefs came up to Lula and
me. They asked us to leave. Well, we did not particularly mind, at least Lula seemed half asleep. I had
about eight *mille* of winnings in my pocket so we went.
Lula went back to her apartments. I stayed out late
because I was always foolish, spent some of the money
and gambled away a good deal of the rest. The next
morning the police were knocking at my door. They
had found Lula, too, although she was miles away
from me. We were offered our railway tickets to
wherever we liked to go but we were bidden to leave
the city before two o'clock, which is the time the casinos
open. We went to Juan. We handed in our passports.
The officials who had welcomed us so courteously a
few moments before returned them with a little shake
of the head. They regretted they were unable to offer
us cards for the *Salle des Jeux*. No explanations. I
lost my temper — quite uselessly. That was the end of
it. The money drifted away. I decided then there was
only one hope and that was Monte Carlo. We had no
money left. I forgot what a coward I have always been
and I set out to rob you, sir. Lula waited at Beaulieu.
Now she is here, I am here, and you are there, and instead of robbing you, you have given us a wonderful
dinner and all I have had to offer you in return has
been a true story, not one word of which will you believe."

Besserley turned his head to the divan. He met
Lula's eyes and although he was not usually clumsy
he dropped his cigar. He stooped and picked it up,

181

savagely threw it into the fireplace and stood with his back to the room.

"No," he declared, "I do not believe a word of it."

Then he heard that quiet, wonderful laugh from behind, full of music, full of irony, full of something a little more mysterious.

"You do not?" she asked.

Baron Domiloff, head of the casino in Monte Carlo and an intimate friend of Besserley's, adopted precisely the attitude which the latter expected. He became a little inattentive towards the end of the recital. He remembered something else he had to do and sent a telephone message. He came back full of apologies. He was uncertain where Besserley had left off but he heard him patiently to the end.

"Well, what is it that you want me to do, *mon ami?*" he asked.

"Give these two tickets for the Sporting Club and come and stand by my side."

"They can have their tickets for the Sporting Club, naturally," Domiloff consented. "I will come and watch your Egyptian miracle for a few minutes with pleasure."

Domiloff was as good as his word. He obtained their *Cartes d'Entrée* from the bureau and then, as the roulette was not yet in full swing, he took them into the bar and sat with them while they had tea. He made several efforts to draw Lula into conversation but she seemed to have turned into a figure of stone whenever he spoke to her. He was observant, however, and he saw that utterly changed light in her eyes when she turned towards Besserley and it puzzled him. Completely and entirely incredulous as he remained, he was beginning to anticipate with pleasure those few minutes at the table. What he did not understand was his failure to win even a smile from this curious-looking yet in her way beautiful child. He asked himself uneasily, when the time arrived for them to commence their experiment, whether really she had some uncanny power of knowing the truth, whether she realized that he had never spoken a word to a woman in his life that was sincere, that he had accepted their adulation as tribute and that for the first time he knew he was understood. She was touching Besserley's arm, looking up at him as they walked around the room. Domiloff laughed cynically to himself. He could not remember the time when he had felt for anyone of her sex what he felt at that moment for the girl who so complacently ignored him.

Places were presently found at a suitable table for Gilbert and Lula. Besserley and Domiloff stood side by side behind. A quarter of an hour passed before anything happened, during which Gilbert lost quite half of the pile of jettons which Besserley had placed before him. Then the girl inclined her head very slowly towards him.

"The number?" she asked.

"Thirty-three," he told her.

She looked towards the croupier, who had thrown

more than one casual glance in their direction. This
time she caught his eyes. Besserley and Domiloff, both
watching, saw that the man seemed to change colour.
Someone spoke to him and he appeared to be deaf.

"Thirty-three," the girl whispered softly to herself
without moving her head.

The croupier at last looked away. His voice was almost raucous as he leaned towards the wheel.

"*Faîtes vos jeux, Messieurs!*" he invited.

Besserley had a queer fancy, all of a sudden, that
everyone had changed into dummies, that the Sporting Club was a dolls' house, that the whole thing was
unreal. Then before he had thrown off the idea the
wheel was spinning, the ball had fallen, the croupier
was announcing the number.

"*Trente-trois — noir — impair et passe.*"

Domiloff stood for a moment motionless. He leaned
forward and watched Gilbert's stake which they were
preparing to pay. He glanced at the ball, he glanced
at the croupier. Few realized that he himself was a
man of amazing imagination which he kept all the
time under stern control. Perhaps in those few seconds
he, too, was walking in another world.

"You are quite a mascot, young lady," he said, the
faintly sardonic note a little forced this time.

She turned her head slowly, giving him plenty of
opportunity perhaps to realize the beauty of her soft
white neck. For the first time she looked at him.

"You think so?"

It was all she said, but Domiloff, too, had seen the

mystery and drew back a little breathless. The game went on. Gilbert staked and lost. The girl herself threw a few louis on from his pile — won a little and lost a little. Then she sat still for a few moments.

"The number?" she whispered presently.

"Fourteen."

She looked as though carelessly down the table. The croupier moved in his seat. He turned to speak to the chef, he leaned over as if to speak to a client but all the time he did in the end what his impulse had been to do when the girl opposite had first murmured the number. He exchanged that long uneasy glance with her. Her eyes for a moment, as they had been before, were distended — almost unnaturally so. Her lips moved. He bent over the wheel.

"*Faîtes vos jeux, Messieurs*," he invited.

Gilbert covered the fourteen with hundred-franc plaques. There was a little ripple of excitement amongst the people as they realized that he had almost reached the maximum. The ball was spinning. Domiloff idly remembered the many books he had read in which this tense moment was commented on. The players watched — the ball spun — the gamblers' fingers twitched — little indrawn breaths were taken at that final click. The ball had fallen. The croupier leaned forward.

"*Quatorze — rouge — pair et manque!*" he called out.

There was apparently just that little buzz of interest which always occurs amongst the onlookers when a big stake is won, but there was also a greater and more furious emotion working. Domiloff was a strong man and he pulled himself together.

"Will you wait for me?" he asked.

Besserley inclined his head. Domiloff walked swiftly to the other side of the table. The croupier was whispering to the chef. He touched the former on the shoulder.

"Come to my office," he begged.

With the croupier following close behind, Domiloff walked down the room exchanging greetings here and there. He dismissed his clerk and secretary and locked the door as soon as he and the croupier were alone together.

"Mario," he insisted, "tell me the exact truth. A thing has happened which I have never seen before. Two numbers have turned up with your spinning which have been previously announced by a player."

The man was shaking like a leaf. He dabbed at his forehead.

"The thirty-three and the fourteen," he admitted. "I know, sir."

"You spun as usual?"

"Absolutely, sir."

"Were you conscious of anything — different?"

The man was silent. He was trembling in every limb. Nevertheless he looked Domiloff in the face.

"I can tell you only this, sir," he said. "Just before I spun the wheel for both those numbers I caught a look from the young woman opposite. If you think I

am mad, sir, I cannot help it. I knew at once that I
was not myself. My arm was tingling all the way to my
finger tips. She was telling me which number and I
could not even see it myself. I simply knew that I was
obeying another influence. If you look on the wheel,
sir — the chef spoke to me — my fingers were per-
spiring when I touched it. When I spun I knew that
the number the young man by her side had backed
would turn up. I could not stop it. I spun as usual.
The number turned up both times."

"As a matter of form, Mario," Domiloff continued,
and his voice sounded to himself hard and dry and
unnatural, "I shall ask you the obvious question. You
were not in any way in league with the girl; you have
not found out the secret which has mocked the whole
world — how to control that wheel?"

"Neither I nor anyone else, sir," the croupier declared. "God knows I speak the truth. I turned with
her eyes on me and I knew what number was going to
turn up, but that was all I knew."

"You had better ask to be relieved, Mario, for a
little longer than your ordinary time," Domiloff said.
"When you return, those two will not be there. Before
you go will you present my compliments to General
Besserley and ask him if he will bring his friends here
at once."

The man withdrew. In a few minutes one of the in-
spectors knocked at the door and ushered in Besserley
and his two companions. Domiloff motioned them to
seats.

"Will you give me your *Cartes d'Entrée,* please," he asked the girl and the young man.

They produced them. He tore them in two. Then he drew a bunch of keys from his pocket.

"Mademoiselle," he said, "you appear to possess a gift which would have an injurious effect upon the finances of the *Société* if we were to give you continued power to exercise it. You are requested not to enter these rooms again or to enter the casino. Will you tell me what sum will compensate you for your promise to leave this place without delay and never to set foot in it again?"

Lula looked up at him, but there was nothing in any way unusual in the smile upon her lips or the gleam in her beautiful eyes.

"It is such a nice place, this," she sighed. "Must we really go?"

"You must indeed," was the firm reply.

She turned to Besserley and Domiloff, who was watching her, felt the conceit which had been the partial inspiration of his life shattered. The light which was shining in her eyes was something altogether different. It was the light which had come from the secret places.

"Where shall I go to, General Besserley?" she asked sadly. "For Gilbert it is easy. He is a man and every pleasure spot in the world is the same to him — but I am alone and I do not love solitude in these crowded places."

Besserley made what was probably the effort of

his life, but even then he was not wholly successful.

"Mademoiselle Lula," he answered, "I can only recommend you to go back to where you came from and God knows where that may be!"

"I will tell you, if you wish to know. Many nights before I left Egypt I slept in the desert. I have slept even at the feet of that great mistress of solitude — the Sphinx. Perhaps, if I go back, she may tell me more of her secrets."

One could almost hear the seconds beating themselves out during the silence that followed. Besserley had lost his wholesome colour. His face was grey and drawn. He stood like a figure of stone.

"I cannot offer you any advice," he said.

The silence was again prolonged. Then the girl turned slightly away with a long sigh. She had apparently accepted her sentence.

"Money," she murmured, "it is hard to think of. What shall we say, Gilbert? You must have the same as I have, but it is understood that we part at the doors here."

"Two hundred and fifty thousand francs each," Gilbert proposed.

Domiloff threw bundles of notes upon the table.

"There are fifty thousand in each of those," he pointed out. "Five for you — five for the young lady."

They all bent over the table. The girl remained icily indifferent. She gathered together her five bundles and dropped them into her bag. Gilbert was shaking all over as he filled his pockets. Domiloff relocked the safe.

"Besserley —— " he began, turning round.

But Besserley, who had faced most known dangers in the world, had fled from the unknown.

IX

A HOPELESSLY wet day, a slight tennis elbow, and a temporary lack of inspiration for his Memoirs, drove General Besserley, of the Château de Villandry, out of sheer boredom into an enterprise which he had many times contemplated, but never accomplished. He started wandering over the great house which he had purchased some years before from the lawyer who was winding up the estates of a very famous French family.

The central part and one wing of the Château were fairly familiar to him, but the east wing, which had been added about the sixteenth century, he had scarcely even glanced at. There was a library here of old books, the crabbed French and Latin of which, however, defeated him. Everywhere the odour of the worn calf-leather bindings, the faded tapestry and ancient furniture spoke of the gentle progress of the years. He pushed open one of the gabled windows, looked up and down admiring the pinnacled tops of the shapely spire of the little chapel. He moved on towards it, descended the stone steps to the ground floor and hesitated. It seemed impossible that this part of the building was inhabited, and yet he was suddenly conscious of an aromatic and very pleasant odour of cooking. He continued his progress, however, and to his surprise found himself walk-

191

ing upon a luxurious strip of ancient, but fine carpet. Outside the door of the room adjoining the chapel he hesitated for a moment. Then he turned the handle and entered, thereby receiving a shock from which it took him several minutes to recover.

It was a very delightful apartment. Nearly every piece of furniture in it must have been hundreds of years old. There were flowers about the room, and there was no longer any doubt as to that smell of cooking. A round table was drawn up towards the wood fire, and a small man with healthy red cheeks and a paper-covered volume propped up in front of him was seated before a very inviting-looking repast. The remains of a partly dismembered chicken were on a silver dish and his own plate accounted for the rest. There were vegetables in silver dishes and a dust-encrusted bottle of wine in a cradle. The little man, who was in the act of raising his glass to his lips, stared at Besserley, and Besserley stared at him. The consternation of the former grew with the seconds.

"May I ask," the intruder enquired, "whom I have the pleasure of entertaining in this remote corner of my house?"

The man rose to his feet. He was inclined to be tubby and his expression was bland and genial, or rather it would have been if at that moment amazement had not practically stupefied him. Now that he was standing, Besserley realized that he was somewhat sombrely dressed for a country district in unrelieved black.

"I — you have forgotten me, *Monsieur le Général.* I was about here often arranging the books when you first took possession. Since then we have seen nothing of you in this part of the Château. I am Andrew Mason and took the place of the resident chaplain during Mrs. Rosenheim's brief occupation of the Château."

"Took the place of the chaplain?" Besserley repeated. "I am afraid I don't quite understand."

The little man was visibly disturbed. He looked around him helplessly. Then, with a very discreet gesture, he dropped the napkin he was holding over the paper-covered book he had been reading.

"I came over here from the United States with Mrs. Rosenheim," he explained timidly. "I am the founder of the sect to which she belonged."

"Sect! What sect?" Besserley demanded.

Andrew Mason coughed.

"In my teachings," he explained, "I avoid the use of the word religion so far as possible. My doctrines are designed to do away with the necessity for any form of superstition. I try to teach those of my followers with whom I come into touch to live creditably in this world of which we know something, rather than to indulge in dreamy discourses of the — er — unknown."

"Then you are not a priest or anything of that sort?" Besserley asked.

"I belong to no established form of religion, sir. I am here to prepare people to die by teaching them how to live."

"And do I understand that you are a member of my household, Mr. Mason?"

"That is so, sir. I stayed on after Mrs. Rosenheim's sudden death. I made friends with many of the villagers and no one seems to have thought of disturbing me."

"You live here?"

"Naturally. I do not take up much space and there are many empty rooms. I have my bedchamber, this apartment where I usually take my repasts, and the sitting-room and library in which I prepare my discourses and interview the more enlightened peasants who wish to consult me about their difficulties. I have fortunately been blessed with the gift of tongues — in other words I am an accomplished linguist."

"Do I — excuse me, but I am a little confused," Besserley proceeded. "Do I support you, Mr. Mason?"

"You certainly do to a limited extent, sir," was the latter's acknowledgment. "It is a very small sum, but there are, of course, the offerings from those who have found it worth while to listen to my teachings."

"The people living round here, you mean?"

"Yes, sir. You have twenty-nine servants in the house and there are nearly always twelve or fourteen extra in the gardens and the estate. Most of them come to my discourses three evenings during the week."

"But what if any of them die or want to get married?" Besserley enquired.

"That has nothing whatever to do with me," Mr. Mason replied. "There is a very excellent *curé* in the adjoining village who looks after the spiritual needs of his flock. The chapel here is always at his disposition if he requires it."

Besserley pulled a chair towards him and found himself muttering a word of apology. Mr. Mason's manners were deferential, his poise excellent.

"So I am supporting the exponent of a new — er — creed, am I?" he meditated.

"The claim upon your steward is a very small one, sir," Mr. Mason pointed out.

"You — er — make enough to live on though?" Besserley asked with a glance at the luncheon-table.

"Your very admirable housekeeper, Madame Delamain, takes care of that," Mason confessed. "Will you permit me the pleasure, sir, of showing you the church? You will find it in excellent condition. The brasses are kept in perfect order and there are always fresh flowers upon the altar."

"But what have you to do with the church?" Besserley demanded.

"Nothing whatever," Mason acknowledged. "I enter it only as a caretaker. I conceive it to be an obligation upon me to see that it is in fit condition for a service at any time that the *curé* of the village wishes to hold one. The only liberty I allow myself is the occasional use of the organ."

Besserley reflected for a few moments.

"Pray sit down, Mr. Mason," he invited the latter,

who was still standing. "I had no idea of disturbing your luncheon. I trust you agree with me that that Château Pontet Canet of the 'seventy-eight vintage is a beautiful wine?"

"It is too good for me, sir," the little man replied. "It is the kindness of your butler who keeps serving it to me in place of the *vin ordinaire*."

"Proceed with your luncheon, please," Besserley enjoined him. "I will not disturb you more than another minute or two. I see some very beautiful books here. These are yours or mine?"

"They are without a doubt yours, Monsieur," the seeker after truth acknowledged.

"Including these upon the bottom shelf?" Besserley asked, leaning down and picking up a volume of Paul de Koch.

The apple-cheeked little man blushed even a deeper shade of red.

"There are times," he ventured, "when one tries to understand the outlook of the world in which one labours."

"I see," Besserley observed, "one or two other classics of the Montmartre type."

"Monsieur is a man of the world," Andrew Mason pleaded. "He will understand that there are times when spirituality needs an antidote."

"My dear fellow, do not apologize to me," Besserley begged. "You are without a doubt the guardian of your own conscience."

There came from the distance the sound of the

opening and closing of a heavy door, footsteps upon a stone pavement and a sudden note of trembling music. Mason glanced furtively at his patron.

"It is the organist," he explained. "She comes to practise for a little time. Shall I send her away?"

"By no means," was the guardedly gracious reply. "I will look into the chapel."

Besserley opened the big oak door which led down two steps into the small church. There were three beautiful stained-glass windows and some remarkable monuments. From a distant table in the chancel came the strong perfume of lilies. The girl who was seated at the organ commenced to play *Kyrie Eleison.* Besserley remained devoutly silent. The girl, however, who had heard the door open, turned round in a moment. She gave a little cry when she saw who was standing there, slid from the seat and crossed the nave. Mr. Mason descended the steps.

"It is the Monsieur who owns the Château, Mademoiselle," he explained. "He had a fancy to look at the chapel."

The girl curtsied respectfully to Besserley. She was a full-bosomed, pleasant-looking young woman of the peasant class, with bold dark eyes.

"Monsieur does not often come here," she observed.

"I believe on the day I purchased this property," Besserley reflected, "I had a brief glance inside. It is a very charming little church, Mademoiselle. The flowers, I suppose, are your arranging. You also make the music."

He spoke gravely but politely. She looked up, rapidly regaining her courage.

"I cannot propose to come to your services," Besserley continued, "for my faith is of another order. I will not disturb you any longer, Mademoiselle."

He moved away.

"Monsieur —— " she began.

He turned his head. The girl's eyes were seeking his.

"It would be the greatest pleasure in the world, a great happiness indeed, if I were one day permitted to play the organ in the great hall of the Château."

"I will see about it," he promised. "I will not detain you now, Mr. Mason," he added. "I must find my way back to my own quarters. Good morning."

Mason hastened out and opened the door for this unexpected visitor who nodded his thanks curtly. Then he closed it and returned to his neglected luncheon. Beads of perspiration were standing upon his forehead and his hands were trembling. He poured himself out a glass of wine.

"So he has found you out, *mon vieux!*" Mademoiselle said, throwing herself into a chair, crossing her legs and glancing towards the table. "For how long have I not told you that it would arrive one day? Why could you not have paid your respects to him and explained matters?"

"It would have been better," the little man admitted, dabbing his face.

"Oh, but I wish Monsieur — he is very handsome

198

— would let me play his organ in the great hall!"

Mason, who seemed to have lost his air of rubicund good living, sat down disconsolately.

"His manner was a little strange," he meditated. "I am afraid —— " He turned the bottle of wine around to look at the label and groaned. "It is the 'seventy-eight," he muttered. "I told Henri not to bring the 'seventy-eight. The 'eighty-four would have been quite good enough."

Besserley, on his return to his study, sent for the steward, who came at once in a desperate hurry. He was a stout, consequential-looking little man of about fifty years of age. He had been wearing a bowler hat which he fingered nervously as he stood before his patron.

"Monsieur Laval," Besserley said, motioning him to a chair, "I have just discovered that I own a chaplain or someone who takes his place — a man named Mason."

"But yes, Monsieur. He is attached to the household."

"Queer thing that I never heard of it."

"I think you will find that somewhere in the agreement to purchase," Monsieur Laval confided, "there was a mention of the fellow. He was a protégé of the American lady who owned the lease of the Château — Madame Rosenheim. It was her intention to found a new religion. Unfortunately she died before she could get things properly started."

"Why didn't he clear out then?" Besserley asked.

Monsieur Laval indulged in a characteristic gesture.

"He had a contract, Monsieur," he explained. "It could have been broken, perhaps, but one did not think of it. He cleans the church and he looks after the books. He has never presumed to take the place of the *curé*, but he does sometimes, I believe, hold meetings and explain his ideas. For myself I know nothing about all that. I am an infidel. I live as I choose. I suppose the people to whom he lectures give him something in addition to his salary. He has always the look of good health."

"Little bounder — so he ought!" Besserley muttered under his breath. "That will do, Laval. I just wanted to know."

The steward took his leave. Besserley summoned Henri, his perfect butler.

"Henri," he said, "I have just discovered that I possess upon the premises the prophet of a new creed."

"Prophet, Monsieur?" the man repeated perplexed.

"A red-cheeked little man — Andrew Mason he calls himself."

The butler smiled.

"He was attached to the suite of Madame Rosenheim, sir," he explained. "I do not know why the lawyers did not disturb him when you took over — probably the matter was overlooked. He devotes his time to keeping the chapel in order for when *Monsieur le Curé* needs it and he also calls himself, as he did in Madame Rosenheim's time, librarian."

"H'm," Besserley grunted. "His taste in literature seems to be a trifle Rabelaisian. I found him established in a very comfortable apartment next to the chapel and drinking some of that old Pontet Canet that I enquired about the other night, with a very excellent luncheon. I like all my staff, you know, Henri, to be well fed, but I do not provide old and rare wines for them. You have the keys of the cellars. Will you tell me how it is that you have served a wine of that description to my 'librarian' for everyday drinking?"

"Monsieur," Henri protested, "it is not my affair. The meals and the looking after of the librarian are arranged by Madame Delamain personally. She keeps a maid who waits upon him and who brings me a ticket for what wine I am to supply him with. Mr. Mason has a particular liking for the Pontet Canet and Madame is one of the most enthusiastic of his followers."

"This is beginning to be interesting," Besserley observed. "I shall ask you to present my compliments to Madame, and request her to step this way, Henri. Before you go there is just a word I should like to have with you."

"*Mais oui, Monsieur.*"

"I like to see my servants looking happy and as though they were pleased with life. Now I have noticed that for the last few weeks you and Pierre and your second man — Charles I think his name is — are all going about hanging your heads and looking miserable. Is there anything wrong with your posts here? Are you not satisfied?"

The man seemed taken aback.

"But naturally, Monsieur," he insisted. "Never have I been in a place more agreeable or served under a patron more generous. If I am not happy just now — well, sir, it is because of a private misfortune."

"Can I help you?" his master enquired.

The man lost some of his almost classic dignity, approaching thereby the similitude of a human being. He hesitated for some time.

"Monsieur, I have the misfortune to have an elderly father too old for work, and my brother who helps me support him has met with an accident. I have sent what I can of my savings but they are in distress. If I might have a *mille* advanced on account of my salary, life again would be a pleasant thing for me."

"Well, get along to Mr. Slattery and tell him to let you have two *mille*. He can arrange with you how to repay it."

"Monsieur," the man replied, and there was a little break in his voice, "I can never sufficiently express my gratitude."

His master waved him away.

"Do not forget to send Madame Delamain."

Besserley lit a cigarette and glanced at the clock. There was still a half-hour to wait for his luncheon, even for his cocktail before it, and it was still raining.

"I wish that pig of a fellow had not lunched so early," he muttered to himself. "Most deliciously cooked, that chicken . . . Good morning, Madame Delamain."

"Good morning, General," she answered respectfully. "I understand from Henri —— "

"Quite right. Sit down for a moment, please."

Madame Delamain was a woman of fifty years of age. She had silvery grey hair parted severely in the middle, she wore a curious sort of cap copied from an old print of life in the family somewhere about a hundred years ago and her dress was fashioned of some harsh black material that seemed almost capable of standing up by itself. She sat on the edge of a chair and looked at her patron with enquiring eyes. She had been telling herself coming along the passage that this was the second time in her life that she had been summoned to the presence.

"I happened by chance," Besserley began, "to start on a tour of inspection this morning. I stumbled upon a very queer and to me unknown denizen of the Château — Andrew Mason he calls himself."

Madame Delamain sat quite still. She made no comment. Her eyes were fixed upon her employer. She waited.

"Do you know, Madame," he continued, "I had no idea that I was supporting such a person in this establishment?"

"The chaplain of the Château has always been provided with a room here," she said quietly, "and in Madame Rosenheim's time no chaplain being necessary Mr. Mason, who came from the States with Madame, took his place."

"All right," Besserley agreed. "I do not want to be disagreeable about it, Madame, I suppose a caretaker of some sort is necessary, but I have just sent for Henri prepared to dismiss him. No one here has the right to serve the famous vintages of wine, which I have collected with some difficulty, to any member of my staff. As you know, a small portion of my cellar is set aside for the use of the household. It consists entirely of sound wines. I have never expected any of them to drink *vin ordinaire.*"

Madame was silent for a few moments, her eyes fixed upon the carpet. Then she looked up again.

"Monsieur," she said, "you will forgive me to this extent. The matter of wines has never seemed to me one of great importance. Therefore, as Mr. Mason — like you, sir — seems to take very particular notice of what he eats and drinks, I have served him with the best. I have served him, also, with the wine he has asked for."

"You have been at fault, Madame," Besserley pronounced. "Wine like that was not grown and kept and stored for everyday drinking. It is for the cultivated tastes. I myself will give Henri instructions as to what wines may be served to Mr. Mason in future. You may content yourself by looking after his food. I desire, however, that he should not be served on my

Sèvres china or with the glass which I saw upon the table as I came through, nor is it necessary to use for him the Italian linen which my principal guests all admire so much. Is that understood?"

"It is understood, Monsieur."

"Wait one moment, Madame Delamain," Besserley concluded, as she rose to her feet and was turning away. "I wish for no misunderstanding in this matter. You are prepared to obey my wishes?"

"But naturally, Monsieur," she assured him.

She had reached the door when Besserley again stopped her. He was a little puzzled by her demeanour.

"Madame Delamain," he said. "The last time I saw you was, I think, a month ago. You struck me as looking unwell. I offered you a vacation which you refused. I am sorry to say that you look no better. Are you ill?"

"No, sir. I am in good health."

"In trouble?"

Madame Delamain hesitated.

"To a certain extent, sir," she admitted, "I am in trouble. I have a brother who has misled both my mother and myself. He was in an *avocat*'s family and we trusted him. He has gone off to Africa with a great deal of money belonging to us."

"Well, that seems hard luck," Besserley observed. "Is there any way in which I can help you?"

She looked up at him hopefully.

"If Monsieur could advance me a trifle — no, more

than a trifle, say five *mille* upon my salary — it would take a great load from my shoulders."

"Heavens! Why didn't you say so before?" he exclaimed. "You can go to Monsieur Slattery and ask him to advance you five thousand francs and to arrange with you as to the method of repayment."

She hesitated for a moment. Then she turned away.

"You are very kind, Monsieur. I shall not forget it."

Besserley rang the bell, which was promptly answered by Pierre.

"I really rang for Henri but you will do," his master said. "Order the cocktails sent in at once."

"Very good, sir."

Pierre hesitated before leaving the room. Besserley glanced at him enquiringly.

"What the mischief is the matter with you, Pierre?" he asked. "You look as though you were about to attend a funeral."

The valet had the air of one summoning up all his courage.

"May I have a word with you, sir?" he begged.

"Get along with it then."

"It would be a great convenience to me, sir, if you would permit me to draw six months' salary in advance," the man said.

Besserley stared at him for a moment in surprise.

"What, you too, Pierre?" he exclaimed. "I always understood you were a man of means — that you owned property around here."

"I still own some, sir, but one of my ventures lately

has been unsuccessful and I require the money to keep up payments on a plot of land I bought last year. It would be a great convenience to me, sir, if you would allow Mr. Slattery to arrange the matter."

"Well, I suppose I must say yes," Besserley acquiesced. "You can go and get the money this time, Pierre. I do not believe in speculation, though, even on a small scale. You must keep out of that."

"I certainly will in future, sir," Pierre promised, "and I am exceedingly obliged to you."

Besserley waved him away but the man turned back before he had reached the door.

"I beg your pardon, sir. I forgot to tell you that there is a young lady waiting in Madame Delamain's room. She desired me to ask whether she might play the organ in the gallery some time to-day?"

Besserley frowned but he did not hesitate.

"She cannot," he refused. "For one thing I am not sure that the organ is in order and for another I do not like the appearance of the young lady, and I do not want her about the Château. Mr. Mason appears to have given her permission to play the organ in the chapel and she must be content with that."

"I will convey your wishes to her, sir," Pierre said. "I might be permitted to add, sir, that she has not the best of reputations in the neighbourhood."

"I can quite understand that," was Besserley's irritated comment as he shook out his copy of the *Times* which had just arrived.

"I do not wish to interfere with Mason and his

followers," he observed, "but I think it will be necessary for me to have a few words with him before long. That will do, Pierre. Send those cocktails along."

"Very good, sir."

The man left the room. Five minutes later, Charles, the youth who was Henri's understudy, made his appearance. He arranged the tray upon the table and drew the corks of the bottles.

"May I serve Monsieur?" he enquired.

Besserley looked up at him and shook his head.

"There are many things I would trust you to do, Charles," he said, "but not to mix me a dry martini on a filthy morning like this."

Charles withdrew respectfully into the background. Besserley regarded him curiously.

"Are you ill, Charles?" he asked.

"*Mais non, Monsieur*," the youth answered.

"What is the matter with you then? You are like everyone else in the place this morning. Is it the rain that is affecting you? Must have a wet day sometimes."

"It is not the rain, Monsieur."

"Then what is it? Come — speak out. Don't tell me that you, too, are in financial trouble?"

Charles drew a long breath.

"Something like it, I am afraid, sir," he confessed. "I was very foolish indeed. I bought a bicycle promising to pay for it this week. The man trusted me because I was in service here. I went home my usual day last Wednesday and spent the night at my father's house. I shared his room and in the morning when I was packing up to come back all the money I had was missing."

"Charles," Besserley demanded, "how much of this is true?"

"It is just as I say, sir," the boy pleaded. "My father is not a bad man, but he is in trouble. He found that I had the money and he took it."

"How much was it?"

"Seven hundred francs, Monsieur."

Besserley fetched out his pocket-book.

"Look here," he said, "I am not going to send anyone else to Mr. Slattery, but I will advance that on my own account. But remember — if you haven't paid me back in two months — out you go! Understand?"

"I am very, very grateful, sir," the boy assured him. "I promise faithfully to pay you back by that time."

"*Parole d'honneur?*"

"*Parole d'honneur, Monsieur.*"

"Off with you then," his master ordered.

Besserley mixed himself a cocktail with meticulous care, sipped it thoughtfully and approved. He looked at the still streaming window panes but he was beginning to feel a little lighter hearted, notwithstanding the continuance of the inclement weather and a sense of vague irritation at the curious behaviour of the various members of his domestic staff. The announcement of luncheon helped still further to clear away

his gloom. He refused the wine offered to him and
pointedly ordered a pint of Pontet Canet '78. Henri
served it without turning a hair.

The remainder of that long dreary day drifted
away hour by hour in uneventful fashion without
further assaults upon Besserley's pocket. His arm
felt a little better towards evening and he had a
couple of games of squash with the resident professional, and a swim afterwards which did something
to restore his flagging spirits. He dined with an improved appetite and decided to concentrate for an
hour or two on his Memoirs. He worked well and it
was not until half past eleven that he began to collect
his manuscript and turned his attention to his nightly
whisky and soda.

"You need not sit up, Pierre," he told his valet
when he arrived for orders. "I may work for another
hour and I can put myself to bed."

Pierre seemed almost unduly grateful. Besserley
filled his pipe and proceeded with his task of collect-
ing the loose sheets he had completed. About half an
hour later he was conscious of footsteps crossing the
main hall. He listened for a moment and laid down
the manuscript. The footsteps were distinctly audible and the person who was approaching, whoever it
might be, was someone who knew his way about, for,
although the main lights were out, he never faltered
and avoided anything in the shape of a collision. Besserley's right hand rested in his half-opened drawer.

He sat still and waited. He was curious but not in the least disturbed, and it was presently obvious that there was no cause for alarm. The door of his study was pushed a little wider open and the invisible man of the place, as he had once or twice been christened, appeared. It was Phillip Slattery, his secretary.

"Hello, Slattery!" his master exclaimed. "You up at this time of night?"

The secretary closed the door behind him and came noiselessly across the room. He was a small man, quietly dressed in dark clothes and wearing horn-rimmed spectacles. The only frivolity about his person was his thick black hair which had a tendency to curliness.

"I am not intruding, sir, I hope? I wish to have a word with you."

"Go ahead," Besserley invited. "Sit down if you want to. I hope to heavens you are not going to be like the rest of them and want to borrow money," he added in a suddenly suspicious tone.

"The amount I receive from you, sir, as recompense for my work, is too generous, I am glad to say, to make that necessary."

"Well then, what is it?"

"I feel that it is my duty, sir, to ask you to share a discovery which I made a few nights ago."

"What — here in the Château?"

"Here in the Château, sir. If you will place yourself in my hands for a few minutes I think the explanation will become self-evident."

Besserley rose to his feet.

"You are very mysterious, young fellow," he said.

"It is a mysterious business, sir," the secretary replied. "If you will follow me along towards the east wing for some distance I should be glad."

"I will come, of course," Besserley agreed. "You are not going to inveigle me into a secret chamber and blackmail me, I hope?"

A very faint smile parted the young man's lips.

"That is not my intention, sir. It is an act of duty which I am regretfully compelled to perform."

Then for the second time that day Besserley skirted the corridor on the eastern side of the Château, up and down short flights of stairs, through ancient doors until he came to the last lap. Here for a moment he paused, suddenly aware of the sound of confused voices. They came from the room leading into the chapel.

"No service to-night, is there, Slattery?" he asked. "It is not a saint's day or anything?"

"Nothing of that sort," was the whispered reply. "Will you please tread as quietly as you can."

Besserley, who was beginning to be interested, obeyed orders. About two doors from the very beautiful library consecrated to the use of Mr. Mason he stopped short. He listened with his head on one side. The thing was impossible. He took a step forward. Slattery kept pace with him. He listened again. Then he looked blankly towards his companion. There was

something curiously familiar about the strain of
those mumbling voices.

"But what is this that is happening?" he demanded. "I don't understand."

"I thought that you might be a little surprised,
sir," Slattery said. "Now what do you think of this,
if you please?"

They stood just outside the door of the room which
Besserley had already explored that morning. The
secretary turned the handle and pushed it boldly
open. Besserley stood upon the threshold aghast.
There was no longer the least doubt as to what that
murmur of voices and queer little click meant. At the
end of the table where Andrew Mason was seated —
rubicund, prim, precise in his black, semi-clerical attire — was a large roulette-wheel and Mason himself
was just indulging in the usual monotonous chant.

*"Faîtes vos jeux, mes amis. Faîtes vos jeux! . . .
Rien ne va plus!"*

Besserley, to the end of his life, never entirely lost
the memory of that tableau. It had in it all the elements of comedy, swiftly changing into melodrama.
There was something there which could only have
been described pictorially by Hogarth or with the
pen by Rabelais. The change of expressions, even as
he stood there and watched, was almost miraculous.
There was Andrew Mason himself, for instance, at
the head of the table. A few seconds before his right

arm had been around the shoulder and resting gently upon the neck of the young lady organist. He was looking with a smile of pleased approbation at the great heap of counters which had been gathered in by her side, and the neat piles which she was making for would-be customers. Then, still ignorant of the disaster which loomed a few yards away, he turned cheerily to the board, made his routine speech, spun the wheel and dropped in the ivory ball. It was because he was a small man and absorbed in the fascination of his occupation that he had no idea of what was happening. He looked only with a beatific smile at the eager faces around the table. He saw Madame Delamain, whose long nervous fingers were playing with her last few remaining counters. He shook his head approvingly as she dropped on a plaque at the latest possible moment. There was Henri, plastering one of the numbers, a cigarette in the corner of his mouth, an expression carefully copied from real life of the devil-may-care gambler upon his face. Paul, the chauffeur, was being a little stolid about the matter but he held a rake in his hand and once or twice he tapped the plaque which he had placed upon a *cheval*. Charles, making no attempt to hide his excitement, was leaning across the table to see where the ball might fall and turning back every second or two to be sure that his own stake had not been disturbed. There were four or five outsiders whose faces were only half familiar to Besserley, and lastly there was Pierre, standing with his arms folded, a gloomy frown upon his forehead, continually moistening his lips. Fate seemed to have insisted upon getting all that could be got out of that picture, for the staking had been unusually heavy. Nearly everyone was seated with his back to the door and the ball had fallen into its little place before, in the general lessening of the tension, everyone either leaned forward or flung himself back in his chair and the cry which revealed Nemesis in many different notes rippled and spluttered hysterically amongst the group.

Andrew Mason was the one who got the last moment's fun out of his evening. The one number neglected by everyone was zero. He looked round the table and he failed to keep the triumph from his tone.

"*C'est le zéro qui gagne!*" he announced.

And then he realized his doom. The rake which he had been gripping clattered from his nerveless fingers. Blank consternation robbed his face of all its rubicund cheerfulness. He looked like one of the ugly gargoyles fashioned in a spirit of devilry outside a near-by cathedral.

"So this, Andrew Mason," Besserley said, breaking the queer silence at last, "is the way in which you dispense your new philosophy of life!"

The sun shone again on the following morning and Andrew Mason proved himself to be a man of precision. The neat little collection of I.O.U.'s which he left behind was examined and found correct by every one of the recipients. Before luncheon the entire staff of the Château de Villandry were going about their duties with buoyant footsteps and light hearts.

"And what about our domestic High Priest?" Besserley asked, when his secretary paid him his usual morning visit and handed over a miscellaneous roll of notes which had been forced upon him by the various members of the staff.

"He was off before daylight, sir," Slattery confided. "My discovery of what was going on was made at a most opportune moment. Last night was the date he had fixed for the payment of all outstanding I.O.U.'s It seems he had purchased an automobile during the last few weeks and he had told the man at the garage that he was leaving for a tour in the Basque country."

"Alone?"

"I fear not, sir."

"The double-dyed villain!" Besserley muttered.

X

THE DRAMA ON THE SIXTH TEE

BESSERLEY was finishing his luncheon seated at a window table of the golf-club restaurant at Mont Agel. Almost as it seemed on a level with him, the magnificent snow-capped line of the Lesser Alps stretched in spectacular and brilliant panorama, the sun glorifying their whiteness and the blue sky beyond, the amazing background. The air which he had been breathing all the morning was mountain air, with just that sun-warmed touch which mingled so marvellously with the tonic of the snows. He had won his match, as he generally did, and he had lunched excellently, which also went without saying. He smiled across at his neighbour, Count Tenroux, who was himself no mean exponent of the game.

"Sorry you have to go," he remarked. "Couldn't manage another nine holes, I suppose?"

The Frenchman shook his head.

"Impossible, *mon ami.* I have to be in Nice at three o'clock. A little affair of a sale of property in which my wife's relatives are interested."

"Always thinking of money, you French people," Besserley grumbled.

"*Toujours, toujours,*" his vis-à-vis admitted gaily, "but then, if you do not worry about it you lose it, and if you are not punctual you lose it. And so *au revoir* and thank you for the game. My lunch next time, remember."

Besserley summoned the steward and, without lifting his eyes from the bill which had been presented to him, he asked a question.

"What pantomime has arrived here this morning, Louis? It is a travelling show, perhaps, or is it only a picnic of photographers?"

There was something of apology in Louis's smile. It was, as a matter of fact, a rather uncouth little crowd who occupied the large table in the centre of the room, and the one woman, in preordinately large checks, who was at that moment gazing at herself in a mirror which she held with one hand and dabbing herself with a powder puff in the other, was most assuredly of the flamboyant type.

"Cinema, Monsieur," he groaned. "If ever a plague comes the way of a maître d'hôtel these days, who loves to keep his room *comme il faut*, it is always the cinema."

Besserley laid a note upon his bill and permitted himself to glance across at the centre table as he waited for the change. Anyone who was accustomed to his eccentricities would have known that he had chosen to pay with a *mille* note in order that the change should take a little longer to procure and that he should have slightly more time to study the five men and single woman who had attracted his notice. There was little of curiosity and nothing of interest in the regard which he bestowed upon them. The woman, who of her type was good-looking, met his eyes without flinching, and one might even have guessed at the beginnings of a tentative smile at the corners of her lips. The men formed rather a curious combination. Two of them might well have been cinema artists, two others were of a harder and more serious type, and it was difficult to believe that the fifth man, who sat on Madame's right hand, was not a person of some distinction. He appeared to be of early middle age, a fair but not florid type with high cheekbones, clear blue eyes and the weary droop of many disappointments in life revealed in the sensitive mouth. None of them seemed in any way inspired by their surroundings, and throughout luncheon they had exchanged but little conversation. Of their personal belongings, however, they seemed to be especially careful. Four of the men had each carried into the room a brown despatch-case and each kept that despatch-case close to the side of his chair. The metal tripods which the waiter had unsuccessfully attempted to consign to the cloakroom were stowed under the table. At the time Besserley was asking his questions their repast had drawn towards a close and a cloud of blue cigarette smoke was rising above their heads. They appeared to have drunk very little wine but the woman had called for a second brandy with her coffee.

"At any rate," Besserley remarked to Louis, who had brought him his change, "they are unlike most of the cinema people I have come across in restaurants. They are quiet, not to say subdued. What are they going to do with all that paraphernalia — mountain views or a golf match or what?"

Louis shook his head.

"They are a surly crowd, Monsieur," he answered. "They are not people with whom one cares to converse. I shall collect their money and be glad to see the end of them. I thank Monsieur very much."

He departed with a bow. Almost at the same moment, Count Tenroux, wearing his overcoat and carrying his hat, re-entered the room hastily. He approached Besserley's table.

"General," he said, "you would like a few more holes — yes? There is a gentleman below who would like to play nine. He had a card to me but I know nothing of his golf."

Besserley glanced around to be sure that the person in question was not within hearing.

"I am not very fond of playing with beginners, you know, Tenroux," he confided.

The Count leaned a little forward.

"You would oblige me very greatly, *mon ami*," he said. "In fact, if you do not play I fear that I must give up my visit to Nice. I cannot tell you who he is but the person whose card he presented is of some importance. I know nothing, either, I must confess, about his golf. Afterwards I may interest you — say later on at the Sporting."

Besserley nodded.

"I will play with pleasure," he agreed, suddenly feeling a new interest in the proposition. "Is he ready?"

"In ten minutes."

Besserley found his adversary waiting for him on the first tee. He was a man of medium height, a little thickset about the shoulders, with a powerful and interesting face. He wore very well-cut golf clothes and his practice swing upon the tee was a reasonable enough performance. He pointed with his driver to a little crowd in front approaching the first green.

"Something which resembles a caravan has just gone off in front of us," he remarked.

"I am sorry but I was detained for a few minutes," Besserley apologized. "I had to send a message and the telephone seems to be out of order."

His adversary nodded.

"My name," he said, "is Presse — P–r–e–s–s–e. I must tell you frankly that it is not my own, but Count Tenroux is my sponsor. I am paying only a short visit in these parts to find a little repose after a great nervous strain."

"I quite understand, Monsieur Presse," Besserley answered with a sympathetic smile. "Mine, as our friend may have told you, is Besserley and I am a retired American officer. We commence — yes?"

"By all means."

Monsieur Presse drove a tolerable ball, Besserley sliced his a little but they walked off side by side.

"If these people in front get in our way," the latter remarked, "we shall soon be able to pass them. You wish to play nine holes, I understand."

"Nine holes," Monsieur Presse assented. "It will be enough for me. My doctor always says more exercise but I tell him, as I tell myself, that my brain exercises my body. Still, we shall see. Air like this is too wonderful to miss and one needs an excuse."

Two only of the little crowd in front were apparently playing — the woman and the man who had sat on her right hand at luncheon. The other four were plodding away some distance ahead, still carrying their impedimenta. The woman looked around angrily as Besserley's long second dribbled on to the green while she was putting. They apparently missed the next hole and went on towards the third tee.

"Madame probably did not realize that you were playing only your second stroke," Monsieur Presse declared. "No one but an unusual golfer or a professional could have reached the distance you did."

"All the same, I should have waited," Besserley acknowledged. "Tell me, Monsieur Presse, did you take any particular notice of that small crowd? They started from the tee whilst you were there, I suppose?"

"Three of them at least are from Paris," was the thoughtful reply. "The man with whom the woman is playing — well, his face is familiar to me. Also one of the others. To tell you the truth," he went on a little uneasily, "if I had realized that they were on the course I should not have played. I have reasons for, as you English and Americans say, lying low for a day or two and I particularly wish to preserve my incognito and to keep any mention of my presence in these parts out of the journals."

"Too many photographers in the world," Besserley observed with an understanding nod and a glance ahead.

"Quite true," his companion agreed. "When I saw them coming down with those wretched tripods I thought they were going to have the nerve even to ask me to pose. Your honour, General."

From the next tee they saw nothing of the little caravan. When they scrambled down to the fourth, however, they received a slight surprise. The man and the woman were still playing, were already in fact half-way to the hole which was up on a plateau, but the four men with the tripods had disappeared. Presse glanced around cautiously.

"They have taken a short cut to the fifth, perhaps," he suggested. "They are probably preparing to take a picture there."

"I wonder," his partner speculated.

They played out the long hole. Besserley, who by this time had established his superiority over his companion, won it easily and stood for a few minutes looking around. There was no one in sight. He turned to his caddy.

"What has become of the couple in front of us?" he asked.

The youth shrugged his shoulders and pointed ahead.

"I think they are waiting on the tee for the next

hole," he replied. "Perhaps they wish Monsieur to go through."

Presse and his caddy were looking for the former's ball and were well out of hearing.

"Who are these people?" Besserley enquired curiously. "Have they played here before?"

"Never," was the confident reply.

"Did you see them take any pictures?"

"Not one, sir."

Presse gave up his ball for lost and the two men, followed by their caddies, started for the next tee. When they arrived there they found the man and the woman seated on a bench. The former rose and lifted his cap.

"Will you not, if you please, go through?" he invited. "We are indifferent players and I fear that we delay your game."

"We are not in a hurry," Besserley assured him, looking around in vain for the men with the tripods.

"Nevertheless, if you please, sir," the other insisted.

Besserley mounted to the tee and waited whilst his caddy teed his ball. He took up his position and paused to look round.

"You observe," he pointed out to Madame, "that this is in fact a blind hole. The hill in front limits our vision. What about your friends with their photographic paraphernalia? They are out of danger, I hope?"

The woman smiled.

"They are not behind that hill, Monsieur," she assured him. "I do not think that they are in any danger at all."

He pointed to the caddies who were trudging along not yet fifty yards ahead.

"One must wait for them to take up their positions," he remarked. "They go forward to watch the flight of the ball."

"Monsieur is a little nervous this afternoon," the lady observed.

"Not for my own sake," he replied. "It is of my friend I am thinking. He has lost two balls already and is developing a slice. For a golfer with that tendency this hole presents quite a problem."

"But how right Monsieur is," she declared. "I said from the first that Monsieur had an air of intelligence. I was a little afraid of him."

"And I," Besserley told her, "fear nothing but the unknown. I am expecting every moment, Madame, that something will happen to clear up the situation."

Presse, who had been walking nervously backwards and forwards, suddenly broke in.

"I do not understand," he complained, "the nature of this curious conversation which you are conducting with Madame and her partner. What is wrong, Besserley? If we are to go through, why do you not drive? The lady has already invited you to pass."

"Alas," Besserley replied, "she is not even a lady. She is a Princess. Of her partner I know nothing, but I can guess. They have apparently led us here," he went on, glancing around and realizing more than ever how secluded a place it was, "for a little conversation. Can we not have it, Monsieur and Madame, with our cards upon the table?"

The woman laughed and she no longer seemed in the least like anything but a Princess. Her laugh was very pleasant and the mocking light in her eyes seemed to speak of complete self-assurance.

"With our cards upon the table, Monsieur," she repeated, "and our weapons in our hands, apparently," she added, pointing to Besserley's fingers which were creeping under his loose jacket.

"A weapon gives one confidence," he observed, as with a swift movement of the wrist he brought the revolver which he usually kept in his locker, but which he had slipped into his pocket at the last moment, into evidence. "Is your business with me or with my companion and can it be possible that you wish to take our photographs?"

"Our business is with your companion," was the significant reply, "and we have not come here to take pictures. If you wish, General Besserley, you can drive your ball and pass on your way. We have nothing to say to you."

Besserley smiled.

"I could scarcely desert my partner in so barefaced a fashion," he remonstrated.

Presse showed that he possessed plenty of courage, although he must have known that the situation was threatening. He looked at the three keenly. His companion was the only one who appeared to be armed, but neither the lady nor her partner had shown any disquietude at the sight of his weapon.

"Is this by any chance a trap into which I have been led?" he demanded.

"Shall I explain, Eugene, or will you?" the lady asked.

The man by her side shrugged his shoulders.

"You have begun, you had better finish," he said. "You have shown more perception than I. You warned me in the club house that you had your doubts about this gentleman on the tee."

Presse turned angrily towards Besserley.

"I repeat — is this a trap into which I have been led?"

"It begins to have that appearance," was the regretful admission. "It is one into which I have blundered in your company, but what the demands of Madame may be I have no idea."

"You shall soon be told, although it is no concern of yours," she assured him.

"It would perhaps be as well if we got on with the business," Besserley agreed. "If this is to be in any way a secret meeting I must remind you that the next couple may be coming along at any moment."

"I do not think so," Madame replied. "First of all, I did not see anyone prepared to start out to play except ourselves and I was assured by the steward that very few people venture up to the links after luncheon as the mists descend so rapidly. Furthermore, there is now a notice, for which I admit we are responsible, at the foot of the hill we have just climbed — 'The fifth hole is not being played. Please proceed to the eighth.' We are quite cut off, therefore, and no one will come this way."

"Then it appears to me," Besserley suggested, handling without ostentation the little weapon which he had produced, "that I am in command of the proceedings."

"I would not be too sure," the woman warned him. "I realize now who you are, my dear General. We have met before and it is too bad that we have both forgotten."

"Not forgotten altogether, Madame," Besserley insisted. "You may take it as a compliment to your histrionic ability and to your skilful manipulation of the rouge pot, a lipstick and a few other cosmetics that I was temporarily deceived."

She laughed at him pleasantly.

"*Monsieur le Général*," she said, "you are forgiven. I regret, however, that I am now about to hand you over a disappointment. It is not you who are in command of the proceedings. It is this little silver whistle which, as you see, hangs around my neck and is now between my fingers."

She held it up and Besserley regarded it with interest.

"And pray, Madame," he demanded, "what can you do with that little toy?"

"I can summon dangerous and terrible help," she told him, "from any one of the four quarters of the compass. Look there," she went on, pointing to the little plantation on their right, "and there," pointing over her shoulder to a large fragment of rock, "and there," she continued, pointing in front of the tee towards another detached mass of fallen granite, "or behind us. A little out of sight, it is true, but easily to be seen if you wish."

Besserley looked gloomily around and nodded. In two of the directions pointed out he caught the dull glimmer of steel.

"Up to a certain point Madame is right," he admitted, turning towards Presse. "The reason I did not go home with Count Tenroux but elected to play with you was because I wondered what anyone could be doing up here with machine-guns of the very latest type in leather cases which naturally suggest the camera. I happen to have seen one before. A little out of the ordinary shape, you will observe. Still, granting that we have walked into a very cleverly arranged trap, what about it, Madame, seriously? Are you going to shoot down the innocent golfers who pass by, even if they do not try to disturb us in our present refuge, or are you going to turn those weapons on my unfortunate partner and myself because I drove into you at the second? It is a severe penalty."

"*Monsieur le Général*," the woman said sternly, "it dawns upon me now that the reason you have been so unduly discursive since we reached this tee has been simply to gain time. It is a quite useless resort and we have had enough of it. Eugene — proceed."

"Well, I certainly shall not be quite so long about it as General Besserley has been, toying with the preliminaries," the man who had been seated by Madame's side declared with a smile. "*Monsieur le Juge*," he went on, addressing Presse, "four days ago you sentenced to death the man whom you discovered escaping into Switzerland from the house which he rented near Lyons. You made no fuss about it. Neither has the Press, neither has his party. You tried him *in camera* and you sentenced him to be shot next Monday."

"And," Monsieur Presse said coolly, "he will be shot and that will be the end of the Extreme Right. Why do you not call yourselves the Monarchist Party and have finished with it?"

"It would sound unpopular as a mass cry," Eugene explained. "Now I have here a form properly drawn up. It is an order to the Governor of the Prison at Salons instructing him to release at once the prisoner convicted under the name of Marc Ozanne and to give him a safe conduct to England. You will sign that or you will die — not on Monday but now, and upon this spot. As for General Besserley's revolver, he can make use of it just as he pleases but it will not affect the final issue. We did not enter upon this enterprise with any undue anxiety as to what might become of us."

Presse looked at the document laid out in front of him. He looked at the fountain-pen, he glanced at the seal, he took note, too, of the embossed coat-of-arms at the top of the paper. Then he read through the few lines of boldly written matter.

"I wonder where you obtained this official stationery and the seal," he observed curiously.

"Does it matter?" the woman asked. "We could have found more difficult things than that. Sign, *Monsieur le Juge*."

"Sign here, *Monsieur le Juge*," the man by her side echoed.

"And if I do not?"

The woman shrugged her shoulders, then she raised her hand above her head. There was a whistling and a hissing from the trees around and Besserley felt a sting of hot air quite close to his left ear. A few seconds later there was silence once more.

"It is indeed the most wonderful machine-gun in the world," the man whom the Princess had called Eugene explained. "It makes, as you have perceived, scarcely more noise than an air pistol but it does its work with terrible execution. Only six of them were smuggled into Spain but the observer's report was an amazing document."

"I ordered that first shot fired," the woman confided, "only to confirm the fact that death is lurking round the corner if Monsieur 'Presse' is obstinate. The shots themselves were to be two yards over your heads and could be fired with perfect safety."

"One of your men was careless," Besserley grumbled. "There was a bullet a good deal nearer than that to my head."

"That was because you moved at the last moment," the woman continued calmly. "The next time I raise my hand, if one hand is there only, *Monsieur le Juge* will have said his *adieux* to the world. If two hands are raised, the gentleman who is holding the little weapon in front of me will also pass away. That would, I am sure, be a loss not only to all civilized Europe but to the world. I trust, therefore, that Monsieur will either induce his friend to sign this document or proceed with his game of golf — alone. Believe me, he would be much safer half-way up that hill."

"Wait a moment," Besserley begged her. "You are aware, Madame, or rather you can divine as a matter of common sense, that if I should see you stand up and raise two hands, if I were to see you stand up and raise even one, it would become an absolute necessity that I should be guilty of an action which I have never before even dreamed of. I should be compelled to take with me a companion into the next world."

"Well," she decided after a moment's reflection, "I look upon your interference as entirely uncalled for but the decision remains with you, *Monsieur le Général*. I am a Frenchwoman and where millions of men have died for their country so recently, one woman is not likely to be afraid. You know as well as I do — foreigner though you are — that if Marc Ozanne dies there will be a revolution in France. France must have peace even if we others have to seek it in the grave."

Besserley was silent for several moments. He looked across at the white-clad mountains. A great stillness seemed to have fallen upon the earth. They were far away from the land of motor horns and all ordinary sounds. A dog barked from one of the hidden chalets in a cleft of the hills. Away farther inland, where the country grew wilder, they heard the scream of a predatory hawk. Man's grip upon this solitary strip of country seemed to have become relaxed. There was nowhere any movement, whisper or sign of human beings. The Princess' supporter broke the silence, which was becoming almost uncanny.

"It would be well if Monsieur signed," he said with an ominous note of finality in his tone.

"I shall not sign," the Minister of Justice decided. "I am sixty-seven years of age. I have had what is best from life. I will not seek a coward's method of prolonging it."

The other man drew a long breath. He looked at the woman by his side. There was the unheard, unuttered and yet thrilling pause — the prelude of tragedy. Besserley felt tongue-tied. For a horrible moment he had the fear that he had lost the nerves of speech. The moment passed. He held out his hand to the woman with a fiercely forbidding gesture. He turned to Presse.

"*Monsieur le Ministre*," he begged, "let that decision of yours stand for a moment suspended. Listen first, you two — you, Princess, and you, her friend whose identity I decline to know — you are idealists, both of you. I am an ordinary man but often I see truth where others miss it. *Monsieur le Ministre*, listen. Tell yourself for a moment that that sentence has not yet been pronounced. It never should have been pronounced."

"The law of France has decreed it," Presse insisted.

"It is not the law of France," Besserley denied. "It is the law of you and your fellow judges. Marc Ozanne was not sinning against his country, he was sinning against political statutes and man's idea of political expediency."

"Talk of this kind is only wasting time," the Princess declared impatiently.

"Hear me out, I beg of you," Besserley continued without turning his head. "You kill him and pay the price. Your own life, probably mine, who am utterly guiltless, probably the lives also of the Princess here and her companion and her four volunteers. Granted that we are all sacrificed. What happens? There are other heirs to the throne of France. It is simply changing one Pretender for another. So long as there are Monarchists in France there will be a Monarchist prince ready to lead them. Take the broad view. Is a Monarchist a more dangerous man than a Communist or an Anarchist? You cannot hang all the Communists, you cannot shoot all the Monarchists. Keep France in the hands of the moderates. Keep on friendly terms with the Right and the Left. Soothe down the extremists — humour them. Govern as Julius Cæsar or Rienzi would have governed. Do not commit a political murder. Sign that paper, *Monsieur le Ministre*. You know very well that you have not had a moment's peace since you signed the death warrant."

"You, too, are a Monarchist, then!" Presse exclaimed.

"My God, no," Besserley answered. "What business have I with French politics? Listen, I will tell you what I speak for. Common sense, honour and stability in politics and not rash deeds committed one day and repented of the next. Sign the paper, Presse, and let these two go back and carry it to Salons."

Perhaps it was the effect of that particular moment amid those marvellous surroundings with the glow of the sunset afire in the skies and the light evening breeze filling their lungs with the pungent sweetness of the gorse, the mountain herbs and the pines which made Presse decide that life, after all, was good. At any rate, he showed signs of hesitation.

"Madame," Besserley went on, "had you a signal for your four camera gentlemen if the paper was signed?"

"What an inspired guess!" she murmured. "I stand upon the bench — so, and I wave my handkerchief."

"Do it, then," Besserley concluded. "The Minister will sign."

Presse stood for a moment in deep and sober silence. Then he took the pen from the fingers of the other man and signed. Madame waved her handkerchief. Disturbing sounds came at last from the hidden places. They heard the rattling as the machine-guns were fitted back into their cases, they saw the four men converge together and make their way round the hill. Besserley approached his ball and gripped his driver once more.

"My honour, I think," he said.

He swung and achieved the ambition of every golfer who drove from that tee — he carried the hill.

The scattered little company all reached the hilltop about the same time. The Princess gripped Besserley's arm.

"What does that mean?" she demanded.

Close at hand, moving with their long swinging stride, their short rifles on their shoulders and preceded by an officer, a company of *Chasseurs Alpins* were rapidly approaching. The officer reined in his horse as the little party came into view.

"It means that my message was delivered after all," Besserley replied. "Let us congratulate ourselves, Princess."

"Upon what?"

"My — discursiveness, I think you called it."

The Princess hesitated, then she released his arm and laughed.

"You really are an amazing person," she admitted.

Besserley lingered for a few words with the officer, after which the latter saluted and rejoined his men.

The little company swung round the base of the hill and disappeared almost as quickly as they had arrived. Besserley found Presse waiting for him as he turned back. Madame and her friend, with their escort of pseudo-photographers, were in front.

"I must ask you, General," Presse said gravely, "how you came to know of my presence here — if you did know of it. What made you an ally of those others?"

Besserley thrust his arm through his companion's.

"Chance — fortune — whatever you choose to call it has taken a hand in to-day's events," he answered. "I knew not even your name — nothing of your eminence in life. I love adventure and I gathered that something unusual might possibly be on foot because I recognized the machine-guns in those cases."

"You came out to play golf with me in ignorance of the whole affair?" Presse asked incredulously.

"Upon my word of honour that is so," was the frank reply. "Now let me ask you a question. You are a great man in France — you occupy a unique and wonderful position. Do you regret those few minutes back on the outskirts of the wood there? Do you regret that signature and the word of honour which you have given?"

The man who had called himself Presse was silent. His eyes seemed to have strayed away. Perhaps he was watching the fading of the distant hills, the mauve haze which was creeping up the valleys, the one or two glimmering lights. Perhaps he saw none of these things. He might have been back in that grim court room face to face with the haggard yet dignified-looking man whom a few days before he had sentenced to death.

"My friend," he said, "it is not given to everyone to be able to act as I have done on impulse. I had the right and I chose to exercise it. I do not regret what I have done. I thank you even for your interposition. My word of honour has been given and it will be kept. . . . The mists strike cold. A small liqueur before we descend?"

Besserley turned promptly towards the club house.

"You may be a great judge," he declared, "but you are a greater man!"

XI

THE STRANGER AT THE BAR

BESSERLEY, who had found the atmosphere of the baccarat-room in the Cannes casino a little more trying than usual, left the place and, sauntering through the crowded saloons, arrived at the bar. He mounted one of the high stools, made his wishes known to the white-clad servitor, who greeted him with marked respect, and glanced around him in search of acquaintances. That at least had been his first intention but he looked no farther than the young woman by his side. Her eyes met his almost at once. There was something of recognition in them to which he felt that he should have responded. Her features, her soft large eyes, the carriage of her head and a queer atmosphere of reserve which she seemed to create around her were all in a dim sort of way reminiscent, yet for once he was at a loss.

"Good evening, General Besserley," she greeted him.

"Good evening, Mademoiselle," he replied.

His drink was brought to him — whisky in a long tumbler with a blob of ice and the freshly-opened Perrier bubbling invitingly. He glanced from it to the girl's barely-touched glass of champagne. A certain bluntness of manner, seldom apparent but one of his most charming characteristics, asserted itself.

"I would ask you to join me," he said, "but you have

apparently just been served. You know my name. I feel that I once knew, but I am ashamed to say, that I have forgotten yours. Will you enlighten me?"

She smiled.

"You will know it before long," she replied somewhat enigmatically. "I stood behind your chair at the baccarat trying to summon up my courage to tell you about myself. I am in Cannes to speak with you, but it is necessary that we are not overheard."

"I love mystery," Besserley confessed with a smile.

She shook her head gravely, raised the glass to her lips and sipped her wine. Then she slowly turned her head and glanced into the crowded space behind. Besserley followed the direction of her eyes. She looked towards a table at which two men were seated. They were both obviously foreigners — even their dinner clothes were cut strangely, their linen and the fashion of their ties were somewhat unusual, but more interesting than these details was the fact that though they each had a glass in front of them they were doing nothing except watch Mademoiselle.

"Your escorts?" he asked.

She shrugged her shoulders slightly.

"They have an interest in me," she replied. "It is not a friendly one. They follow me everywhere. I wish they would go away. I have already refused to discuss a certain matter with them."

"I have no fancy for interfering in other people's affairs," Besserley confided, "but if there is anything I can do — just a hint perhaps?"

She glanced down the row of stools. The next three or four were unoccupied. They were almost isolated.

"I will remember that if I may," she told him. "You are a very well-known man, General Besserley, but you apparently aim at seclusion. You are on the telephone at your Château, but no one may speak to you unless they know your private number. Your Château stands there for the world to admire but no one may pass your lodge gates without your permission. Your servants answer no questions. Royalty itself is not more inaccessible."

"I have only taken the ordinary precautions to enjoy a certain amount of independence in an overcrowded district," Besserley assured her. "Needless to say I am now regretting their existence."

"A courtier always," she murmured, and he noticed that her lips although sensitive and attractive in their smile were more fully developed than the lips of English or American women. "These moments of tranquillity will not last. There will be people here directly. It is a fact that I wish to speak to you. If you will leave the casino in half an hour and find your way to the east side of the harbour you will see a small motor boat prepared to leave. It is called *The Sunshine*, and it is at mooring number twenty-seven. If you would give yourself the trouble to meet me there it would be a great kindness and I might possibly provide you with what they say is the joy of your life — an adventure, even though it be a trifling one. Will you come?"

Besserley had instincts and he never hesitated.

"Mademoiselle," he assured her, "I shall be there."

She slipped from her stool, nodded a careless good night and passed out of the room. Besserley watched her till she reached the door. She walked with a swaying grace which puzzled him. She carried herself with ease, even distinction. She returned none of the curious glances which in that small nest of boulevardiers were freely bestowed upon her. Besserley turned to the barman who was once more in his place.

"By chance, Charles," he asked, "do you know the young lady with whom I was talking?"

Charles shook his head.

"I have never seen her before in my life, *Monsieur le Général*," he acknowledged. "She came in quite silently, ordered a glass of champagne, of which she has only drunk half, and neither looked at nor spoke to anyone. Decidedly, Monsieur, she is a *jeune dame sérieuse*."

"I am under the same impression," Besserley assented.

At precisely the time stated Besserley made his way along the crowded waterfront and paused before station number twenty-seven, the spot indicated. There was a small crowd, rapidly being re-enforced in all directions, standing on the edge of the quay, apparently watching a newly arrived submarine. There was no sign whatever of *The Sunshine*. Besserley was on

242

the point of leaving the place when he came face to face with a familiar figure.

"Just the man I was looking for," Besserley observed, touching his hat to the Harbour Master. "Can you tell me what has become of a small craft — *The Sunshine?*"

The Harbour Master leaned forward and recognized his questioner.

"I have been asking the same thing myself, *Monsieur le Général*," he said. "I gave her a mooring earlier in the evening. She was there exactly where that queer-looking submarine is. As to what has become of her —— "

A young man in naval uniform broke in rather rudely upon their conversation. He had apparently just disembarked from the submarine and Besserley noticed that he had been talking to the two strangers of whom Mademoiselle had complained in the casino bar.

"Mr. Harbour Master," he said, "I am in search of a small motor boat — *The Sunshine*. I understand she was here close to the berth I have taken up myself."

The official stiffened a little.

"I was just explaining to this gentleman, sir," he answered, "that I had allotted the station you have taken up to *The Sunshine*. She has, however, disappeared. I have no idea whether she has changed her mooring or left the harbour."

He turned his back upon the enquirer and led Besserley to one side.

"What's all this about?" the latter asked curiously. "What sort of a craft is *The Sunshine* anyway and what's the submarine doing here?"

"She came in without warning, General," the Harbour Master replied, "and just now she is not a particularly welcome visitor. I am awaiting instructions concerning her. *The Sunshine* was just an ordinary luxury motor boat — forty-foot type."

"Who is the owner?" Besserley asked.

The Harbour Master looked at his questioner closely.

"To tell you the truth, General," he said, "I have had a hint dropped to me that *The Sunshine* is not to be talked about."

"I was invited on board her to-night," Besserley confided. "I came down to meet someone."

"The lady owner, sir?"

"Yes."

"Then Monsieur knows who she is?"

"I have no idea."

The Harbour Master coughed.

"I am afraid in that case, sir," he said, "I can do no more than reply as I have done and shall to the commander of the submarine — I know nothing about her or why she has disappeared or where she has gone."

"That isn't friendly, Captain," Besserley expostulated.

The Harbour Master laid his hand upon Besserley's arm. He led him a little way down the quay towards the casino. Once or twice he looked round.

"Your boat is lying here, General, isn't she?" he asked.

Besserley pointed her out, a shapely converted trawler of at least two hundred tons, well lighted, with a sailor standing to attention near the gangway.

"Any objection to taking me on board for a moment?"

"Not in the least," was the prompt reply. "I was about to suggest it."

In the saloon, with a whisky and soda by his side, the Harbour Master became more confidential.

"I didn't like it out there, sir, on the quay," he explained. "Too many people listening. That submarine is a queer sort of craft. The authorities will have to deal with her. She is sailing under the new Spanish flag, but there's no doubt about it — she has been in action."

"That's interesting," Besserley admitted. "But at present I want to know about *The Sunshine* and the lady."

The Harbour Master appeared worried.

"All that I know about her, General, is guesswork. I put a few things together in my own mind and I would rather not repeat them but I will tell you this. She is living alone with a maid and manservant on a small island close to Lérin, and every enquiry I have received about her — and there have been many during the last two days — has come from the spies, I call them, of a certain Power with whom we are not particularly friendly just now. What they want with her I cannot tell you. She's got something up her sleeve and they have got something in their minds about her. It is not my affair," the Harbour Master concluded, finishing his drink and picking up his casquette, "and that is all I can say about it. You will excuse me now, General? I must get back to my job."

Whereupon the Harbour Master took his leave and Besserley realized that he was just as far off as ever from being able even to make a guess at the identity of the strange lady who had fled from her rendezvous. The night, however, was young.

It was about half past eleven when Besserley, who had just decided to spend the night on board, heard footsteps on the gangway and a familiar voice hailing the *Sea Spray*. Almost immediately the steward announced a visitor.

"Mr. Hatherwaite, the American Consul, sir."

Hatherwaite was following close behind. He exchanged greetings with Besserley.

"Hope I am not disturbing you," he said. "We had a cable come through from Washington and as I knew the *Sea Spray* was in the harbour I brought it down myself."

"Very good of you. Sit down. Another glass and some ice, steward."

"I can't stop more than a minute or two," the Consul explained. "My people are over at the casino, and I am my own chauffeur. Will you just run through the message and see if it is a matter in which the Consulate is concerned?"

Besserley opened the despatch and glanced at its length with a frown.

"It is in our private secret-service code, Hatherwaite," he confided. "I'll let you know in the morning if there's anything official."

The Consul nodded.

"Is it true that one of these mysterious submarines from the Spanish coast has turned up here?" he asked.

"It's here all right," Besserley acquiesced, "flying the new Spanish flag, the Harbour Master told me, and in a pretty battered condition. I shouldn't have thought they would have risked bringing it in, but that's not our business."

"Sleeping here to-night?"

Besserley assented.

"If there's anything in this message I'll see you in the morning," he repeated. "Frankly I do not think that it is Consular business at all. It is in a private code which we have not used for years and I expect it will take me all night to get the sense of it."

The Consul took his leave. It was dawn before Besserley had finished his decoding. He felt thoroughly worn out when he threw himself down to sleep for an hour or two, but he was no longer in doubt as to the identity of the mysterious lady.

At eight o'clock in the morning Besserley was awakened by his steward.

"A letter brought on board marked 'Immediate,' sir," he explained. "I thought I had better wake you."

Besserley tore open the envelope and read the note.

To General Besserley.

  Sir,

  Please to come over at once to this small island. The bearer is the pilot of The Sunshine *and he will show your man the channel. It is very difficult. Come in any boat you can find or your own if it is there, but come quickly.* The Sunshine *must be left in Cannes Harbour. It will be watched and followed when it leaves.*

  Please forgive that I was compelled to run away last night. I will explain.

Z.

Besserley wasted no time. He telephoned up to his Captain and engineer. In five minutes the engines were throbbing. In a quarter of an hour they were leaving the harbour. Half a dozen men on the deck of the submarine were watching them. *The Sunshine,* which had apparently just come in, was tied up in the next berth. Besserley hurried the French pilot who had brought the note into the chart-room.

"We want to make Little Lérin," Besserley informed the Captain who was at the wheel. "This man is a pilot if you need any advice."

The Captain leaned over the side.

"It depends upon the tide, sir," he said, "but if the

pilot knows the passage we can make it all right. It would be safest to land from the launch if you are thinking of going ashore."

Besserley nodded. It was only a short journey and he was still in his pyjamas.

"Bath, shave, clothes and glasses," he told the steward. "A cup of tea as soon as I come on deck. Send the lad aft and tell him to look out and report to me if we are followed."

The man hurried off. A few minutes later he knocked at the door of the bathroom.

"There's some sort of a craft left the harbour coming out on this course," he announced.

"Tell the Captain full speed ahead," Besserley ordered.

A quarter of an hour later he was on deck dressed and shaved. He looked at the white trail left by the oncoming boat and smiled.

"How are we for stores?" he asked the steward.

"Nothing we are short of that I can remember, sir," the man replied. "We have a reserve supply of everything. I have started the refrigerator already."

Besserley drank his tea and munched a piece of toast. He then strolled into the chart-house.

"We're nearly there, sir," the pilot told him. "The tide is on the turn already. It will be best for you to land from the launch."

Besserley was thoughtful.

"We shall see," he decided. "I don't want to leave the boat if I can help it."

There was a slight sea running and some indications of the east wind. They had left the pursuing craft some distance behind but Besserley watched her thoughtfully. He blew his whistle and the boatswain promptly appeared.

"Put a blank shell in number four gun," he ordered, "and have a live one handy."

The man looked astonished but he saluted and hurried off. Besserley turned his glass upon the small island they were rapidly approaching and gave a little grunt of satisfaction. On one of the scattered rocks upon the beach a woman was standing, watching their approach. Behind her was the small house which was the only habitation.

"How near can you get to that rock?" he asked, pointing it out to the pilot.

"Right up to her, sir," was the prompt reply.

"Could we take the lady off without landing?"

The pilot looked at him suspiciously.

"If she is willing to come," he replied.

"Take her in as near as you can, then," Besserley ordered. "There is a strange boat following us. What will happen to her if she tries to make this passage?"

"She will have the devil's own luck if she makes it, sir," the man answered. "There are three hidden rocks barely a couple of feet under the water. We have passed one of them already."

Besserley returned on deck. He watched the American flag fluttering in the strengthening breeze. He was running a risk and he knew it. He turned once more towards the rock. It was the woman of the casino bar who stood there, her figure clearly outlined now. Her hands were raised above her head. There was something almost heroic in her poise.

"And to think that I never guessed who she might be," Besserley muttered to himself.

They drew nearer and nearer. Besserley stretched out his hand for the megaphone which the steward by his side had been holding.

"We are coming right in alongside," he shouted. "Can you make the jump? Wave your hand if you hear me."

She waved her hand and sent a long fluttering cry out to him.

"I can do that!"

Wind and tide were both favourably against them. The difficulty as they drew nearer was to keep that gulf of deep sea from suddenly widening as their speed slackened. Suddenly Besserley felt a little thrill. The woman was climbing down what seemed to be a descent of sheer granite. She set her feet in invisible places; it almost seemed as though she clung to its worn crevices with the palms of her hands. They were within a few yards of her now. Everyone on the boat was silent and breathless. She measured the distance coolly, clinging with legs and feet to the surface of the rock. Then, at precisely the right moment, she let go and took her leap. Besserley caught her in his arms. Together they swayed for a moment against

251

the side of the wheel-house, then with a little laugh and breathing quickly she caught the rail.

"Here I am!" she exclaimed. "Have I done what you wished?"

"Marvellously," he answered.

He shouted orders to the pilot. The man leaned out towards him. A few rapid sentences were exchanged. Besserley nodded and turned to his passenger.

"Look here," he said, "I understand a little of this business now. Do you know anything about that submarine that came in?"

"I know that there are men on board whom I do not wish to meet," she confided. "They are friends of the two who were watching me. I am afraid of their race. I am afraid they would interfere with what I wish to accomplish."

"Well, they are coming up behind," Besserley told her. "They followed us out. They cannot catch us when we get clear but we have to go dead slow for a few minutes."

"Do the best you can," she begged, "to get me away from them."

He nodded and stepped back into the wheel-house. When he returned she was standing calmly leaning against the rail looking almost as little perturbed as when she had stood by his side at the casino bar a few hours before.

"Now tell me what it is that you wish, Princess," he said. "If you say the word we will keep you on this boat and I can land you wherever you like."

"Thank you," she said with a brilliant smile. "I prefer that. I will be landed at Devanna."

"Devanna?" Besserley repeated. "Where the mischief is that?"

"It is the port, the chief port, of my country."

He stared at her for a moment in surprise.

"It will take us five days," he told her. "You haven't a maid, clothes or anything."

"I can manage," she assured him serenely. "I prefer not to return to Cannes — not even to my island. Neither is safe. You do not wish to take so long a voyage? Remember, you must not call at any port. If it is necessary you may go to Malta."

"What about this man we have on board whom you sent to me this morning?" Besserley asked.

"He is of no account," she replied contemptuously. "I have paid him for a month and for the hire of his boat. He will accompany us wherever I choose. The decision is yours to make. I wish to go to Devanna."

"Nothing in the world," Besserley assured her with a twinkle in his eyes, "will give me so much pleasure as to escort you there."

She smiled slowly.

"You are a very gallant man, General Besserley," she acknowledged.

He had a reply ready but it died away upon his lips. They were edging their way down the narrow channel when suddenly just outside in the lee of the island he caught sight of the submarine.

"Clever devils!" he exclaimed. "They guessed we

253

would come out this way so they have kept to the open sea."

"Will they sink us?" she asked calmly.

Besserley smiled.

"Somehow I don't think they will even try," he said. "However, we shall soon know."

The Captain hurried out of the wheel-house.

"The submarine that came into Cannes last night is outside — dead ahead, sir," he announced. "She is signalling us to stop."

"You will excuse me for a moment?" Besserley begged.

"I will come with you," the girl replied.

Besserley stepped into the wheel-house, took up one of the telephones and shouted an order below. Then he talked briefly but very much to the point to the pilot who was still at the wheel, and to his Captain. Finally he took up the megaphone and stepped out on deck. Very soon they were within thirty or forty yards of the submarine. An officer stood on the bald, unprotected hull and shouted.

"Heave to, *Sea Spray!* We are sending a boat to board you."

"What the devil do you mean by giving us orders?" Besserley rejoined. "We are going straight ahead."

"We have affairs with the lady on your boat," the officer insisted. "It is necessary that you stop."

"We have no intention of stopping," Besserley announced.

There was a moment's pause. Another officer

crawled up from the interior of the submarine. He took the megaphone.

"General," he called out, "we ask you courteously to receive some officers who wish to speak to the lady you have on board."

"Spanish officers, I suppose?" Besserley scoffed. "I see you are flying the Spanish flag."

"That is not your affair," was the prompt rejoinder. "We order you to heave to."

"I refuse," Besserley replied. "We are going right ahead. What are you going to do about that?"

"Sink you," was the angry retort.

Besserley leaned over the side.

"Let her go, boatswain!" he called out.

There was a sudden report from beneath, a violent oscillation of the ship. One of the two officers on the submarine nearly slipped into the water in his start. The other was holding on to the conning tower. They seemed too amazed for words.

"That was a blank charge," Besserley informed them politely. "We've a live shell ready now. I can put you at the bottom of the Mediterranean in a few seconds if you try any more of those threats. No," he added, waving his arm, "you wouldn't have time to swing round the machine-guns even. You are asking for it. Do you want it?"

There was no reply. Besserley turned to the Captain.

"Full speed ahead!" he ordered. "Ram the submarine if she's in the way."

"You have no right to carry guns," one of the officers shouted, his voice trembling with passion.

"And you have no right to fly a flag that isn't the flag of your country," Besserley answered. "I have a licence from the United States Government to carry two guns and that is our flag and you had better turn round and go back to where you came from."

A further group of the officers came up from below. They were all shouting and gesticulating incoherently. The *Sea Spray* was tearing through the water now at twenty knots and increasing her speed every minute.

"I don't believe they have a torpedo left," Besserley grunted. "Anyhow, they will never be able to get into position to fire it. Swing her round to starboard, Captain," he added, raising his voice. "Keep her lined away and due south-east."

Besserley's surmise was probably right. In a quarter of an hour the submarine was nothing but a little grey smudge upon the waters and they were doing their thirty knots straight ahead.

"I would suggest," Besserley proposed as he laid down the glasses, "that we descend to the saloon and have our coffee."

She linked her arm through his.

"You really are quite a wonderful man," she said.

Seven days later, in the magnificent natural harbour of Devanna, the Princess Zilla and General Besserley watched the approach of a perfectly modern

area. As a consideration we
of a million dollars and al
million dollars a year so l
territory. There are a few
not to grant concessions t
you are to provide us with a
for which, of course, we sl
be fixed upon later. The ot
there. They are not impor
for half an hour and you
your advisers have not ur
I hope that you will give n
with me and that you will l
documents. I shall have a
to pay over and I shall si
behalf of my Government.'

The King rose and bowe
but gracious in manner.

"You have spoken like
"We wish to grant you th
cated with our envoy in 1
us to approach you. We
another direction, but my
task of searching you out
ceeded. We shall be glad 1
is what my country needs
to defend herself. We s
General Besserley."

Besserley took a brief l
out on the deck and his st

and quite new motor boat in which were seated several men in picturesque uniform.

"That is my brother, the King," the Princess pointed out. "The man on his right is his Chief Counsellor and the one on the left is the head of the army."

"Fine-looking fellow, your brother," Besserley commented. "Seems to me, Princess, we have talked this little show of ours almost to shreds but there is one question I have never asked you."

"There are several which I began to think you had forgotten," she remarked demurely.

Besserley's fingers tightened upon her arm.

"The one I was thinking of at the moment was intensely practical," he told her.

"Please ask it me now, then," she begged.

"Why were you so determined not to sell this land or grant these concessions to your neighbors?"

"I will tell you why," she replied. "There are indeed several reasons. For one thing neither I nor my brother trust them. For another thing I think as soon as they landed here and began setting up works, and digging, they would feel once more that lust of conquest that has become almost like madness to them. I think, to tell you the truth, the end of it would be that they would take over our country. We lease you the land, we grant you the concession, you plant your flag and I think that there is no one who would interfere with it."

"You are quite a modern young lady, aren't you?" Besserley observed.

"You forget," sh
have travelled. I hav
Vienna and I have i
than my brother ev
soldier and he woul
tapping her forehea
they come."

She waved her ai
the steps and embra
tongue for a few n
serley and present
where champagne a
Afterwards Besserl
ments which he ha
spoke a few plain

"Your Majesty
the mountain Kin
profitable should s
nations. It has bee
which I received fr
is an enormous dei
for nickel, and wi
been discovered a
which you seem t
other substances v
duce a metal hav
want it for airpla
ferent purposes. (
with red lines.
country the right

of almost uncanny prescience, appeared presently
with a single glass and a cocktail shaker. Besserley
grinned as he watched the pouring out of the yellow
liquid and tasted it with approval. In many respects
it had been a trying morning.

Luncheon, the signing of agreements, the handing
over of the draft, the discussions for the commence-
ment of the work — everything went smoothly. The
King took a fancy to his host and Besserley, face to
face with a new type, was interested and impressed.
Evening came and the motor boat waited. The business of farewells, very ceremonious and somewhat
lengthy, commenced. In the end the Princess Zilla
drew Besserley on one side.

"Is this," she asked wistfully, "to be the end of
our friendship?"

"The end of our friendship, I trust, will never
arrive," he answered. "I must go back to Cannes. I
shall probably have to go over to the States on this
affair, for there will be trouble to be faced even though
we are on the safe side. You will see me here again
later, and it will be a great happiness to me."

"No more than that? I, too, should like to go to
America."

He shook his head.

"You are too romantic," he sighed. "America would
never impress you."

"You do not imagine," she asked sadly, "that I

shall ever be contented to live in this wild, barren country?"

"There will come a time," he reminded her, "when someone will take you away from it."

"Now listen to a really immodest speech," she whispered, leaning a little towards him. "I wish very much that it were you who were taking me away from it."

He kissed her fingers. The King in the background was growing impatient.

"My dear," he said, "wishes have sometimes a strange gift of fulfilment, and memory, too, is a thing worth having."

"Zilla!" her brother called out.

Her eyes were full of tears when she threw back her head.

"The French fashion, then," she begged.

So he kissed her on both cheeks and she went away with her face uplifted, and in the boat, as they took their places, her laugh seemed the heartiest and her gaiety the most natural, but when the *Sea Spray* swung round the point and disappeared she had no more words.

XII

THE woman, icily detached, a strange statue of misery, stood in the gloom of the frowzy, poverty-stricken apartment suffering dumbly. It was the man who talked — a fierce figure of suppressed anguish, the lines of unhappiness deeply engraved in his drawn, haggard face. The only evidence of vigorous life remaining was the glitter of his deep-set eyes. He was clad in the soiled garments of a workman. His masses of black hair looked as though they had not been disturbed by brush or any other form of attention for days. His shirt was open at the throat and collarless, his shoes were only half laced up. He was slouching over a common little writing-table littered with sheets of paper and he was still grasping the pen in his hand though the ink in it had run dry. There had been a moment or two's silence, the silence of exhaustion. He recovered his breath and continued.

"Money — what could it give me? Drink. I can cadge that. At the café there is always a glass of Pernod for the man who can tell them that he lived for sixteen years on Devil's Island and earned his liberty through killing two of his fellow prisoners to save the life of a gaoler."

"You must still have a heart," she said, "or you would never have interfered."

"I have a heart," he growled, "but not for you, my
262

noble lady. Look at me! Look at the paper hanging down from the walls of my one apartment! Look at my unmade bed! Look at my foul furniture! It is all the home I have. It is no better than my prison cell, but here I have one thing — I can work out my vengeance."

"Are those the Memoirs you spoke of?" she asked, pointing to the loose sheets of paper upon the bare table.

"A part of them," he answered. "Very interesting. I have just finished the story of our first love adventure and our return to the Embassy at night. Your husband was in England. It was later that night you gave me the papers you stole from his room, the papers I passed on to the Austrian in the café on the other side of the river. I was being watched then. You were always safe, though."

The woman raised her head. She had been beautiful in the days of which he spoke. Even now when her hair was grey, her cheeks hollow and terror lurked in her eyes she had charm.

"I can find," she told him, "ten thousand pounds. That is for your Memoirs — and the letters. You could at least live on that for the rest of your life. You could get away from this terrible room."

He laughed raspingly.

"You waste your time," he scoffed. "Get out! Send the police if you will. Tell them I tried to blackmail you. The letters are not here. Other men have written lies in their Memoirs but the letters speak. They are addressed to your husband — the premier Marquis of England, the statesman peer who is to save his country from disaster. They are addressed to him and they will fall into his hands whatever happens to me."

"Ten thousand pounds," she repeated.

"Get out!" he ordered.

The woman went.

Lady Sybil Temperley-Budd, Marchioness of Bideford and wife of England's most distinguished statesman, travelled southwards from Paris in state, as was her custom. In the adjoining coupé of the *Train Bleu* was her maid, and on the other side her secretary. The *Chef de la Gare*, wearing a silk hat for the occasion, conducted her to her compartment. The Ambassador himself arrived in time for a few words of farewell. Nevertheless, when the moment came when she was alone the smile faded from her lips. The dinner which was served in her compartment remained uneaten. She spent a long and weary night, her eyes hot, that vision of horror always before them. After so many years of success and happiness, so many years of a sheltered and beautiful life, it seemed incredible that she should be faced with such a disaster. Then she thought of that long stretch of time and remembered the broken man who had lived through those same years in agony of mind and body. Once or twice in the night she shivered uneasily. Apart from the terrible position in which she herself was placed for the first time she found herself looking down unwillingly into that grim hell of suffering which had made so vile a thing of its victim. . . .

With the daylight and the sunshine some portion of her courage returned, yet when her old friend, General Besserley, rose to greet her in the beautiful library of his Château a few hours later it was difficult for him to keep entirely concealed the shock which her appearance caused him. He welcomed her warmly, however, established her in a comfortable chair, ordered tea and loosened her furs with his own fingers. All the time he talked as casually as possible.

"So often lately I have thought of writing you," he said. "Your husband's successes, especially during the last five or six years, have been wonderful. You must be a very proud woman, Sybil."

"I am the most miserable creature on earth," she confided. "I am in a state of mental agony and like all selfish women I have come to beg for help from the strongest person I know. There are so many who have done that," she sighed.

"Tell me about it," he enjoined.

She told him the story, told it as she thought rather well, yet towards the end she felt that she must have failed somewhere. The sympathy in his kind eyes seemed to have died away. He was looking at her almost sternly.

"Lionel Tresillian," he said meditatively. "Yes, I remember him. When your husband was Ambassador he was the second secretary — very popular before his disappearance, a very delightful young man, a favourite with everyone. Full of life, too, and courage. Now you tell me that he has returned — a blackmailer — that he has threatened you. Wasn't he once a little — forgive me, Sybil — a little in love with you?"

"He was — or thought he was," she admitted. "You would not think so now if you heard him talk — if you saw him!"

"Let me see," Besserley went on, "I must understand. This Austrian — Ferdinand Krashki ——"

"I have told you," she interrupted. "I have confessed. He was my lover."

"And Tresillian — this boy, Lionel?"

"He hoped to be. If you saw the miserable wreck he is now, Samuel, you would understand the horror of that half-hour I spent with him. What am I to do? He works now in rags and filth at these hideous Memoirs in which he threatens to disclose the whole story of those days. The letters I wrote to him — God, what foolish things a woman can do! — they are at the bank addressed to my husband. One of them speaks of the papers I stole from the Embassy safe for Krashki."

"Did Tresillian know that you loved Krashki? This may hurt, Sybil, but I must understand."

"He guessed — perhaps I should say, feared," she acknowledged. "He hoped that it was only an infatuation. He never realized the whole truth until the trial."

Besserley leaned back in his chair. His eyes had left the room. He was gazing out across the forest of pines.

"Tresillian made no defence, if I remember rightly," he reflected. "He was tried by a French court and sent to Devil's Island for life. Let's see, that must be seventeen years ago."

"He saved the life of a gaoler last year during a mutiny of the convicts. They set him free some months ago."

"You say that he refused your money?"

"He laughed at me. He must be starving, Samuel. I never dreamed that a human being could live in such filthy surroundings. He — Lionel Tresillian — for whom nothing in Paris was good enough! Now he is like a wild animal. God knows what I went through in that room!"

"God also knows," Besserley reminded her, "what he must have gone through during the last seventeen years whilst you were the uncrowned queen of your country."

She crossed the few feet between their chairs, fell on her knees and clutched at his hands.

"Why are you so strange?" she cried. "Don't you realize that unless something can be done I am a ruined woman? My husband's career of which we have both been so proud is ended. I should be discarded, robbed of everything in life. Why are you so hard? Are you not sorry for me?"

She gripped his arms but they were unyielding.

"Sybil," he said, "I have always been a truthful man. I have helped many people in my time, people for whom I have had sympathy. In this matter my sympathy is not with you — it is with Lionel Tresillian."

She seemed on the point of collapse. A curious surprise was struggling with a spasm of pain in her face. She still clung to him.

"What is Lionel Tresillian to you?" she sobbed. "Here am I — we have been friends all our lives — you see me face to face with ruin and you say that your sympathies are with the man who threatens me!"

Besserley rose slowly to his feet. His arms went around her, it is true, but only to replace her in her chair. He walked slowly up and down the room. Her eyes followed him.

"You were my friend always!" she cried. "You mean that you will not help me, you will not go to him or to the law, to some of those great people you know who might sweep him away — back even to Devil's Island —— "

"Stop!"

His interruption frightened her. His whole attitude appeared to her astonishing.

"I do not understand," she faltered.

He shook his head sadly. It seemed to her incredible but she fancied there was a shade of contempt in his expression instead of the sympathy which she craved.

"Write down Tresillian's address," he told her. "I will go to Paris to-night. I will see him."

She sprang up. Hope returned to her. Her eyes were lit with gratitude.

"You will help me then, Samuel?"

"You might put it like that. My desire is to help Tresillian. In doing that I shall probably be helping you. That will not be my chief aim. It sounds ungallant, Sybil, but it is the truth. I think that you have been a very wicked woman. I think that your present attitude is — shall we say — lamentable?"

"To think," she muttered, "that I should hear this from you — my oldest friend!"

No one who had known him in any of the crises of his life would have recognized Besserley, the great philanthropist, in those minutes. The lines of his face had all tightened, his eyes had lost their kindly gleam.

"You have not touched your tea," he reminded her. "Too bad. I shall order some wine for you and some fruit. You must tell me about the family."

There was a moment of dignity which perhaps in later years saved her memory. She drew herself upright.

"If you will be so kind as to order my car," she proposed. "I perceive that my mission is a failure."

He touched a bell and gave the order.

"Sybil," he said, and though his tone was somewhat softer there was no relaxation in his attitude, "your visit may turn out to be a success. If it is you will owe your gratitude to my sympathy for the man whom you have wronged — not to me."

"I think that you are crazy!" she exclaimed.

He shook his head.

"I am seeing you as you are. You can look upon me as the conscience which is holding up the mirror in which some day you too will see the truth," he told her.

The apartment in which the man was still writing his Memoirs had none of the facilities for ensuring privacy. There was no concierge in the lodge below, there was not even a bolt upon his door. Tresillian looked up fiercely at the sound of the knock and glared across the room as his visitor calmly entered.

"Who the hell are you and what do you want?" he demanded.

"An old acquaintance," was the quiet reply. "What a filthy den this is!"

Tresillian laid down his pen. He rose to his feet.

"Get out of this!" he ordered.

"When I get out," Besserley rejoined, "I shall take you with me."

Tresillian stared at him.

"My God!" he exclaimed. "It's Besserley!"

"Right! Glad you've kept your memory at any rate. Mind if I smoke?"

"Get out of this," Tresillian repeated, only this time in a less truculent tone.

"Not a chance."

Besserley produced a leather case and lighted a cigar. He offered the case to Tresillian who stood staring at him like a statue.

"What do you want here?" the latter demanded.

"A great deal," Besserley replied. "I can see it won't be easy. My immediate intention is to wrap you up in my overcoat, conduct you downstairs into a car and take you to my flat."

Tresillian's laugh had something in it of insanity.

"You always were a meddling ass," he sneered. "How are you going to get me out of this — carry me?"

"I could do that if I had to. When you have lived a Christian life for a month I should not like to try it, though," he went on. "Better smoke one of these cigars whilst we are talking, Lionel."

Tresillian looked at the case and shook his head. He was suddenly himself again for a moment.

"I should be sick," he groaned. "I have had no food for twenty-four hours."

"No money?"

"Heaps if I cared to go and look for it. I'm busy."

"Writing your Memoirs, I understand."

Tresillian shook with rage.

"So that woman has been after you!" he shouted. "I expected something of that sort — or the police if she had the courage. Damn her, and damn your interference! Look here, I am prepared for something of this sort." He opened a creaking drawer of the table and drew out a revolver. "I spent some of my good-conduct money on this," he confided. "Six cartridges all in their places, and I can still shoot pretty straight. I am not to be interfered with, Besserley. I am a dangerous man. I would shoot you as soon as swat a fly upon my table. Get out!"

Besserley watched his cigar smoke curl up to the ceiling.

"Get it off your chest, Tresillian," he said. "You would never shoot a man sitting down, and I will stop here until you are sane again."

"Read some of those pages," the other mocked. "You will see I am sane enough. Beautiful English. I have not lost the trick of writing. My publishers are going to make a lot of money. Would you like to read a page?"

"I wouldn't touch the filth!"

"Stop that!" the man at the writing-table growled. "Perhaps you will say what you have come for then?"

"For one thing to remind you that you were born a gentleman," was the calmly spoken reply. "Gentlemen do not write Memoirs like yours. They don't send a woman's letters to her husband. They don't do either of these things if they are in their right mind. If you did them the person you would shoot afterwards would be yourself. I am going to remind you of a few things."

Besserley paused. Tresillian took no advantage of the fact. He remained dumb.

"Your father is dead," Besserley went on. "Your mother is still alive. Your sister has two splendid sons. There is a good deal of family left — Tresillian family — my friend."

"You are going to be surprised in a minute," Tresillian warned him. "If you don't get up I shall shoot you sitting."

Besserley rose slowly to his feet, knocked the ash from his cigar and crossed the room. For the first three paces he looked straight into the barrel of the revolver. As he reached the table, though, the weapon went clattering on to the floor as the man who had been gripping it collapsed. Besserley bent over him and patted him on the back.

"I'm sorry, old chap," he said. "I've got to be firm, you know. You have been through a lot. Now I am ready to humour you."

He took off his overcoat. Tresillian scarcely resisted when he wrapped it around him. Besserley collected the loose scraps of paper and thrust them into his pocket.

"Come on," he directed.

Tresillian made one more effort. He was trembling — a strange, stricken figure looking out of the voluminous garment in which he was enveloped.

"For the love of Heaven leave me alone," he begged. "I have just this to do and nothing else."

"You will do the nothing else first," was the calm rejoinder. "Come on!"

Afterwards, in looking back on those days, it sometimes seemed to Besserley an easily-won victory. Yet it was not. There were times, indeed, when he almost despaired. There were times when Tresillian in wild moments trod again the borders of insanity. Yet always the thing progressed. From the first era of ready-made clothes, constant baths, the services of a watchful valet, Tresillian passed on to the coiffeur's visit, the hosier's, the tailor's, the long hours in the open air. Paris was soon left behind. They wound up at the Château where Tresillian, daily putting on flesh, daily regaining his poise and bearing, came back into the momentum of life. He played tennis or squash every day; he began to take an interest in current events. He sailed Besserley's smaller boat until the wind tanned his cheeks and the sun burned his body. He even spoke of the past. Besserley had one agonized letter from Sybil. He answered it shortly.

My dear Sybil [he wrote],

I think that you may discard your fears. Tresillian, if he is not entirely cured, is on the high road to recovery. Since the day I found him up till the present we have not mentioned your name.

I will let you know when I think the time has come when I can talk to him of your affairs without fear of his losing his reassembled grip on life.

It was during her week as lady-in-waiting at Balmoral that Sybil wrote back.

Do not think, my dear friend, that I am ungrateful, but do something, can't you, to set at rest for ever these horrors which constantly haunt me?

Of course, I am glad that you have made a sane man of Lionel, but sane men can carry grudges and hatred as well as lunatics, and I know from your attitude that even you, my friend, believe that Lionel has cause for his hatred.

Besserley took up his pen and replied promptly.

My dear Sybil,
If you are still sometimes tormented by these fears of yours you must remember that you have had a marvellous and amazing escape. The danger grows less every day. Tresillian is almost himself again and when that time arrives he will scorn the thought of his Memoirs and sending those letters to your husband just as he will discard with contempt his thoughts of you.

To that letter the woman found nothing to say and a few nights later what Besserley had been waiting for came to pass. He and his guest were sitting out enjoying the warmth of the spring evening, the languorous air, heavy with the perfume of the fruit blossom and flowering shrubs, the moon shining gloriously on the glittering waters of the Mediterranean. Tresillian was smoking his cigar with the air of a man who has lived and suffered but who has at last found content in life. He suddenly turned towards his companion, drew from the pocket of his dinner jacket a little packet and handed it over.

"The written stories of what one man has done for another, dear friend," he said with very vital seriousness, "are nowhere to be found except perhaps in the pages of the Bible. It is a hard task to speak — it is a hard task for me to try to tell you what I feel. I do not think that I shall ever try, yet I think that you will always know. Those are the letters which frightened Sybil almost to death. Destroy them when you please. Of the Memoirs I shall not speak. You know as well as I that they will never be written. You have saved my body and you have saved my soul. No man can do more than that. In a week's time I shall go back to Tresillian, a hard life just at first, perhaps, but they have kept the place in case I was ever heard of, and my lawyers have been preparing the way for my reappearance."

"That's fine," Besserley declared heartily. "What I wanted to have you tell me, Lionel, was just this. There is to be no more brooding. You are forty-one years old and you don't look a day more. You walk and speak and act as a Tresillian should. You have learnt to forget."

"I have learnt to forget and I have forgotten," the other assured him. "No one but you could have taught the lesson. There was genius as well as Christianity about the way you set to work. You did it. I am what they call reconditioned," he added with a smile as he sipped his brandy, "yet I don't feel in the least second-hand."

Besserley smiled into the night.

"You have made a good job of yourself," he acknowledged. "Remember, you have the best years of your life to come."

"The best years of my life to come — yes," Tresillian murmured.

He fingered for a moment the nosegay of violets in his buttonhole and leaned a little farther forward in his chair. He pointed over the tops of a belt of pine trees.

"Tell me," he asked, "what is that light upon the sea?"

Besserley followed the direction of his finger.

"That," he told his guest, "is the reflection from the lights of Monte Carlo."

"I should like to go there," Tresillian confessed a little bluntly.

"Nothing easier," Besserley assured him. "I have only stayed away because I was not sure that you felt up to it yet. To-night if you like?"

Tresillian glanced downwards at his soft-fronted shirt. Besserley smiled.

"Monte Carlo will welcome us as we are," he declared. "A dinner suit with an occasional white waistcoat and buttonhole is all she demands for the most formal occasion."

"Then I should like to go to-night," Tresillian acknowledged.

A car was at the door in ten minutes. Very soon from the heights of the Middle Corniche they looked down upon the Rock of Monaco with its load of fantastic buildings and upon Monte Carlo with its blaze of lights and at the firmament of stars shining from the bosom of the hills beyond. Besserley watched his companion's sensitive face closely.

"Never been here, have you, Tresillian?" he asked.

"Never," was the brief reply.

"The place," Besserley observed, "is a law unto itself. Sometimes I think that even the people themselves have passed out from under the ordinary jurisdiction of living. Still, it has its fascination."

They passed down by the flower-girt gardens, paid a brief visit to the bureau of the Sporting Club and wandered into the rooms. Tresillian seemed a little dazed but interested all the time. Besserley, watching him now, thought the end of his task had arrived.

"Want to play?" he asked.

Tresillian shook his head.

"To-morrow — the next day, perhaps," he said. "It is just the people. I cannot believe that this is the world I was finding it so easy to leave."

Besserley, as usual, was beset by friends. Although he tried all he could to keep his guest by his side he looked around presently to find himself alone. It was not until later in the evening that he discovered Tresillian. He was standing with one hand upon the high chief's chair of a roulette-table gazing with fixed eyes at a girl on the other side who was watching the play. The girl was wearing a very simple though modish black dress of some soft clinging material buttoned up to her neck with a little band of white around the collar, a gown which was intended by its Parisian creator to designate the modified distress of a not inconsolable widow. His eyes were fastened upon her, and Besserley understood only too well the reason. He threw a few jettons upon the board and stood by Tresillian's side. He made some light remark and the latter came back to earth.

"You see how complete my recovery is, dear friend," he said. "I recognize the likeness and I feel nothing but admiration."

Besserley took the bull by the horns.

"It is more than an ordinary likeness," he said. "The girl you are looking at is the Vicomtesse de la Falaise. She lost her husband last year. She is the daughter of the Marchioness of Bideford."

Tresillian made no reply. Every now and then he showed some faint interest in the game and threw even a few counters upon the board, but most of the time he was watching the girl.

"Do you know her?" he asked Besserley.

"Certainly I do. She was at the Château with some other young people only a few days before I went to Paris."

"You would present me?"

"Nothing easier."

They strolled round to the other side of the table. The girl greeted Besserley warmly. He presented Tresillian.

"A friend of mine who is staying with me," he told her. "He is convalescing after a long illness."

The girl was duly sympathetic. Other friends greeted Besserley and he allowed himself to be led away. It was not until an hour later that he found Tresillian and his new friend seated on a divan in the bar. Tresillian looked a little self-conscious as he greeted his host.

"Are you in a hurry?" he asked. "We thought of going below for a little time. The Vicomtesse is going to show me the new dancing."

Besserley nodded assent as though it were the most natural thing in the world.

"I will look you up there presently," he said. "I have promised the director I will play baccarat for an hour."

Some acquaintances claimed the girl's attention. She excused herself temporarily and Tresillian led Besserley on one side.

"Tell me," he said, "how long has she been a widow?"

"About a year," Besserley replied.

"The Vicomte?"

Besserley shook his head.

"A mistake," he confided briefly. "He was a weakling, a gambler. They were already separated before his death."

Tresillian indulged in one of his rare smiles.

"Am I a weakling, my dear friend?" he asked. "Even though she were the daughter of Satan's wife she is the only woman I have ever wanted to marry."

"Amongst her friends," Besserley said earnestly, "there has never been anyone more beloved than Victorine de la Falaise. She is a young woman for whom I have always had a great affection. No one in the world could complete your cure so thoroughly or in such picturesque fashion."

Tresillian looked around to answer her summons, and there was an absolutely human eagerness in his expression.

"Wish me luck, my friend," he whispered, "for if it comes I am already cured."

Not that night but a very few nights afterwards the cure was well on its way towards completion. A month later the chaplain of the British Embassy in Paris supplied the last touch. The Marchioness of Bideford, who read the announcement in the *Times*, was never wholly able to account for the momentary sense of irritation which it caused her. She reread Besserley's letter, however, and indulged in a sigh of resigned satisfaction. After all, as she explained to the world, Victorine and she had never understood one another, and perhaps, she admitted to herself, Tresillian was safer as one of the family.

THE END

BOOKS BY E. PHILLIPS OPPENHEIM

Mr. Oppenheim's published books, including the four omnibus volumes, total 151. Some of them have never been published in the United States. All those which have been issued here (by Little, Brown and Company) are starred. Titles now in print in the United States, either in the regular editions or cheap editions, are double-starred. Some others are available in English editions. Dates refer to *first* publication in book form, whether in England or the United States.

NOVELS

Mr. Oppenheim has published in all 109 novels, of which 12 have not been published in the United States (unless in pirated editions). Five of his novels appeared under the pseudonym "Anthony Partridge"; these are marked †.

EXPIATION. 1887

A MONK OF CRUTA. 1894

THE PEER AND THE WOMAN. 1895

*A DAUGHTER OF THE MARIONIS. 1895

FALSE EVIDENCE. 1896

A MODERN PROMETHEUS. 1896

*THE MYSTERY OF MR. BERNARD BROWN. 1896

THE WOOING OF FORTUNE. 1896

THE POSTMASTER OF MARKET DEIGHTON. 1897

THE AMAZING JUDGMENT. 1897

*MYSTERIOUS MR. SABIN. 1898

A DAUGHTER OF ASTREA. 1898

*AS A MAN LIVES. 1898

*MR. MARX'S SECRET. 1899

*THE MAN AND HIS KINGDOM. 1899

*THE WORLD'S GREAT SNARE. 1900

*A MILLIONAIRE OF YESTERDAY. 1900

*THE SURVIVOR. 1901

*ENOCH STRONE. 1901
(English title A MASTER OF MEN.)

BOOKS BY E. PHILLIPS OPPENHEIM — NOVELS

*A Sleeping Memory. 1902
   (English title The Great
   Awakening.)
*The Traitors. 1902
*A Prince of Sinners. 1903
*The Yellow Crayon.
   1903
*The Betrayal. 1904
*Anna the Adventuress.
   1904
*A Maker of History.
   1905
*The Master Mummer.
   1905
*A Lost Leader. 1906
The Tragedy of Andrea.
   1906
*The Malefactor. 1906
   (English title Mr. Win-
   grave, Millionaire.)
*Berenice. 1907
*The Avenger. 1907
   (English title The Con-
   spirators.)
*The Great Secret. 1908
   (English title The Se-
   cret.)
*The Governors. 1908
†The Distributors. 1908
   (English title Ghosts of
   Society.)
*The Missioner. 1908
*†The Kingdom of Earth.
   1909
   (English title The Black
   Watcher.)
*Jeanne of the Marshes.
   1909

*The Illustrious Prince.
   1910
*†Passers By. 1910
*The Lost Ambassador.
   1910
   (English title The Miss-
   ing Delora.)
*†The Golden Web.
   1911
*The Moving Finger. 1911
   (English title A Falling
   Star.)
*Havoc. 1911
*†The Court of St. Simon.
   1912
*The Lighted Way. 1912
*The Tempting of Taver-
   nake. 1912
*The Mischief Maker.
   1913
*The Double Life of Mr.
   Alfred Burton. 1913
*The Way of These
   Women. 1914
*A People's Man. 1914
*The Vanished Messen-
   ger. 1914
The Black Box. 1915
   (Novelization of photo-
   play, published by Gros-
   set & Dunlap.)
*The Double Traitor.
   1915
*Mr. Grex of Monte
   Carlo. 1915
*The Kingdom of the
   Blind. 1916
*The Hillman. 1917

BOOKS BY E. PHILLIPS OPPENHEIM — NOVELS

BOOKS BY E. PHILLIPS OPPENHEIM

**THE GALLOWS OF CHANCE. 1934

**THE MAN WITHOUT NERVES. 1934
(English title THE BANK MANAGER.)

**THE STRANGE BOARDERS OF PALACE CRESCENT. 1934

*THE SPY PARAMOUNT. 1934

**THE BATTLE OF BASINGHALL STREET. 1935

**FLOATING PERIL. 1936
(English title THE BIRD OF PARADISE.)

**THE MAGNIFICENT HOAX. 1936

(English title JUDY OF BUNTER'S BUILDINGS.)

**THE DUMB GODS SPEAK. 1937

**ENVOY EXTRAORDINARY. 1937

**THE MAYOR ON HORSEBACK. 1937

**THE COLOSSUS OF ARCADIA. 1938

**THE SPYMASTER. 1938

AND STILL I CHEAT THE GALLOWS. 1939

**SIR ADAM DISAPPEARED. 1939

**EXIT A DICTATOR. 1939

**THE STRANGERS' GATE. 1939

BOOKS BY E. PHILLIPS OPPENHEIM

SHORT-STORY COLLECTIONS

Of these 37 collections of short stories, 26 of which have been issued in book form in the United States, most of the volumes are series with sustained interest in which one group of characters appear throughout the various stories.

*THE LONG ARM OF MANNISTER. 1908
(English title THE LONG ARM.)

**PETER RUFF AND THE DOUBLE-FOUR. 1912
(English title THE DOUBLE-FOUR.)

*FOR THE QUEEN. 1912

*THOSE OTHER DAYS. 1912

MR. LAXWORTHY'S ADVENTURES. 1913

THE AMAZING PARTNERSHIP. 1914

*AN AMIABLE CHARLATAN. 1915. (English title THE GAME OF LIBERTY.)

BOOKS BY E. PHILLIPS OPPENHEIM

MYSTERIES OF THE RIVIERA. 1916

AARON RODD, DIVINER. 1920

AMBROSE LAVENDALE, DIPLOMAT. 1920

HON. ALGERNON KNOX, DETECTIVE. 1920

*THE SEVEN CONUNDRUMS. 1923

*MICHAEL'S EVIL DEEDS. 1923

*THE INEVITABLE MILLIONAIRES. 1923

*THE TERRIBLE HOBBY OF SIR JOSEPH LONDE. 1924

*THE ADVENTURES OF MR. JOSEPH P. GRAY. 1925

THE LITTLE GENTLEMAN FROM OKEHAMPSTEAD. 1926

*THE CHANNAY SYNDICATE. 1927

*MR. BILLINGHAM, THE MARQUIS AND MADELON. 1927

*MADAME AND HER TWELVE VIRGINS. 1927

*NICHOLAS GOADE, DETECTIVE. 1927

THE EXPLOITS OF PUDGY PETE. 1928

CHRONICLES OF MELHAMPTON. 1928

THE HUMAN CHASE. 1929

JENNERTON & CO. 1929

**WHAT HAPPENED TO FORESTER. 1929

*SLANE'S LONG SHOTS. 1930

*GANGSTER'S GLORY. 1931 (English title INSPECTOR DICKENS RETIRES.)

**SINNERS BEWARE. 1931

**CROOKS IN THE SUNSHINE. 1932

**THE EX-DETECTIVE. 1933

**GENERAL BESSERLEY'S PUZZLE BOX. 1935

**ADVICE LIMITED. 1936

**ASK MISS MOTT. 1936

**CURIOUS HAPPENINGS TO THE ROOKE LEGATEES. 1937

**A PULPIT IN THE GRILL ROOM. 1938

**GENERAL BESSERLEY'S SECOND PUZZLE BOX. 1939

BOOKS BY E. PHILLIPS OPPENHEIM

OMNIBUS VOLUMES

*CLOWNS AND CRIMINALS:
  The Oppenheim Omni-
  bus. 1931
containing
  MICHAEL'S EVIL DEEDS
  PETER RUFF AND THE
    DOUBLE-FOUR
  RECALLED BY THE DOU-
    BLE-FOUR
  JENNERTON & CO.
  AARON RODD, DIVINER
  [The cheap edition con-
    tains only the first four
    books]
  (English title THE OP-
    PENHEIM OMNIBUS:
    Forty-one Stories
containing
  MICHAEL'S EVIL DEEDS
  THE DOUBLE-FOUR
  MR. BILLINGHAM, THE
    MARQUIS AND MADELON
  AARON RODD, DIVINER)
**SHUDDERS AND THRILLS:
  The Second Oppenheim
  Omnibus. 1932
containing
  THE EVIL SHEPHERD

GHOSTS OF SOCIETY
THE AMAZING PARTNER-
  SHIP
THE CHANNAY SYNDI-
  CATE
THE HUMAN CHASE
SECRET SERVICE OMNIBUS.
  1932
containing
  MISS BROWN OF X. Y. O.
  THE WRATH TO COME
  MATORNI'S VINEYARD
  THE GREAT IMPERSONA-
    TION
  GABRIEL SAMARA, PEACE-
    MAKER
**SPIES AND INTRIGUES:
  The Oppenheim Secret
  Service Omnibus. 1936
containing
  THE WRATH TO COME
  THE GREAT IMPERSONA-
    TION
  MR. BILLINGHAM, THE
    MARQUIS AND MADELON
  GABRIEL SAMARA, PEACE-
    MAKER

TRAVEL

**THE QUEST FOR WINTER SUNSHINE. 1927